W9-BLL-829

THE COMIC BOOK WAR

JACQUELINE GUEST

© Jacqueline Guest, 2014

All rights reserved. No part of this publication may be reproduced, stored in a retrieval system, or transmitted, in any form or by any means, without the prior written consent of the publisher or a licence from The Canadian Copyright Licensing Agency (Access Copyright). For an Access Copyright licence, visit www.accesscopyright.ca or call toll-free to 1-800-893-5777.

This novel is a work of fiction. Names, characters, places, and incidents either are the product of the author's imagination or are used fictitiously. Any resemblance to actual persons, living or dead, is coincidental.

Edited by Laura Peetoom
Cover and text designed by Tania Craan
Typeset by Susan Buck
Printed and bound in Canada by Friesens

Library and Archives Canada Cataloguing in Publication

Guest, Jacqueline, author
       The comic book war / Jacqueline Guest.

Issued in print and electronic formats.
ISBN 978-1-55050-582-5 (pbk.).--ISBN 978-1-55050-583-2 (pdf).--
ISBN 978-1-55050-801-7 (epub).--ISBN 978-1-55050-802-4 (mobi)
       I. Title.

PS8563.U365C66 2014   jC813'.54   C2014-900459-1
                                                 C2014-900460-5

Library of Congress Control Number: 2014931277

COTEAU
BOOKS

2517 Victoria Avenue
Regina, Saskatchewan
Canada S4P 0T2
www.coteaubooks.com

10 9 8 7 6 5 4 3 2

Available in Canada from:
Publishers Group Canada
2440 Viking Way
Richmond, British Columbia
Canada V6V 1N2

Available in the US from:
Orca Book Publishers
www.orcabook.com
1-800-210-5277

Coteau Books gratefully acknowledges the financial support of its publishing program by: the Saskatchewan Arts Board, The Canada Council for the Arts, the Government of Canada through the Canada Book Fund and the Government of Saskatchewan through Creative Saskatchewan.

For Lorraine Tourond

Dearest Auntie Queen – your amazing memory
for details of events long past never cease to educate and
entertain me. Thank you for all the hours of tea,
talk and wonderful adventures.

PROLOGUE

---

*IT STREAKED FROM THE FARTHEST REACHES OF AN
UNKNOWN GALAXY – A SILVER SWORD CARVING THE
LIMITLESS NIGHT SKY. OUR HERO STARED, UNABLE TO
MOVE, UNABLE TO HIDE, AS THE BRILLIANT INTERSTELLAR
VISITOR BURNED ITS WAY TOWARD HIM.*

CHAPTER ONE

OUT OF THE DARKNESS

WITH A THUNDERCLAP, it slammed into the earth behind the hill. Robert Tourond saw a cloud of dust and debris explode into the air and adrenalin sent him running – not away, as any thinking fifteen-year-old should have done, but toward the carnage.

Stumbling through the darkness, a glimmer in the distance caught Robert's eye. He slid down a particularly muddy slope and veered in the direction of the beacon.

"Wham! Kablam!" he cursed, hearing fabric tear as his pant leg caught on a jagged rock hidden under the slime.

There was a weird smell in the air, like after a lightning strike, and he figured he was close. Topping a small rise, Robert saw the dry prairie grass blazing and raced over to stomp out the flames.

Coughing from the acrid smoke, he wondered what was going on.

Then he spied it.

There, glowing bright cherry red in the blackened weeds, was a tiny...a tiny *what*?

He glanced up, wondering if those practice air-raid drills he'd thought were so silly had perhaps been needed after all. Was this a piece of a Nazi Messerschmitt BF 109 or a big Junkers 88 that had been targeting peaceful Calgary, Alberta?

He shook his head at the ridiculous idea. Nah, couldn't be. The air-raid warden would have loved the rare chance to sound Wailing Winnie, the warning siren, long before any plane was even near the city.

This was something else, something strange.

Slowly, Robert reached down and gingerly touched what appeared to be a small rock.

"Jeez, Louise!" he yelped, yanking his burnt fingers back from the blistering stone. Taking out his handkerchief, he picked up the pebble. Heat radiated into his hand as he examined his find.

Realization came to him. There was only one thing it could be. It was a meteorite, a piece of the universe, a fragment of a fallen star. Actually finding one was something that happened once in a lifetime – heck, once in a hundred lifetimes! It was worth keeping.

Winding the cloth around the oddity, Robert stuffed it in his pocket, then started back in the direction he'd left his bike. As he trudged through the darkness, an overwhelming need to see the rock again made him stop and dig it out of his pocket. He was sweating and felt a weird tingle as he held his special prize.

The moonlight reflected dully off the heavy pebble's rough surface. It was mesmerizing. When he moved it around, it shot tiny electric sparks into his palm. This was his lucky night. He'd found a small piece of heaven.

Stashing it carefully back in his trousers, he frowned at his torn pants leg. The pants were new and his mother was going to explode when she saw them. It was late, too. He had to get home before she called out the cavalry.

Now, where was his bike? No way would he leave it behind, even if it meant getting the third degree from his mum for being AWOL. Robert looked around. Everything appeared eerily different in the moonlight. Squinting, he saw something odd in the silvery light. There was a piece of fabric caught on a rock and not any old fabric: it was the missing piece of his trouser leg. Hurrying over, he picked up the scrap and stuffed it in his pocket with the meteorite. What a stroke of luck to spot it! He might just be saved from death by angry mother when he got home. Plus it meant his bike was at the top of the nearby rise.

Robert climbed up to the ridge and saw his pride and joy right where he'd left it. He'd always had CCMs before and liked the Canadian-built bike well enough. For Christmas last year, though, his parents had splurged and bought him this top-of-the-line Raleigh three-speed, the greatest bike on the planet. Hopping aboard the sleek green wonder, he sped toward a shortcut he'd discovered that would save him an hour of pedalling. It was faster but also kind of dangerous.

Nose Hill, a high plateau on the northern outskirts of the city, was rugged and in several places the path down was narrow and followed the edge of a cliff. In the daytime you could enjoy spectacular views of the Rocky Mountains to the west. At night, even with the moonlight, he had trouble seeing three feet in front of his tire.

Robert approached a blind bend in the trail. Before he could make the turn, a coyote sprang out in front of him. He veered hard, skidding wildly, as he barely managed to miss the nocturnal hunter. Heart pounding, he decided walking down was way safer for him and his green machine. He pushed it around the corner, and then stopped.

A large boulder loomed in front of him, blocking the path. If he'd ridden around the bend and hit it, he'd have gone over the edge for sure.

Robert squeezed past the obstacle, being careful not to scratch his bike, then appraised the inky sky, now tranquil as a still pond on a summer night. He was enjoying some extraordinarily good luck and it had started with finding his new treasure; a treasure that had come from out there – from the void, from outer space!

He could feel the meteorite in his pocket and, oddly, it still pulsed with heat, like it was happy he'd come along. "And," Robert announced to any passing star that cared to listen, "this little piece of the Milky Way is going home with me!"

CHAPTER TWO

PARALLEL UNIVERSES

SEPTEMBER WAS ROLLING BY, so school was back in full swing. As Robert walked down the hall he noted that, although he was in high school now, everything was pretty much a repeat of last year. Grade ten had the same boring planets in their same predictable orbits. In fact, Crescent Heights High was the very definition of predictable. The jocks still strutted with other jocks, their brawn overpowering their brains. The popular girls still giggled mindlessly as they rated a student's worth based on whether she'd made the cheerleading squad. And the brainiacs still furtively scuttled down the halls, dodging the jocks for health-and-safety reasons and avoiding the females because their genius didn't extend to interacting with that particular alien species.

Robert much preferred the loners. They kept to themselves and didn't crave the spotlight. He could understand that. In the past, if he wanted company, he'd always had his three brothers. Now that they were all overseas fighting in the war, he had something else that was far more satisfying than any phoney clique at school.

His universe was contained in the pages of the comic books he lived for, those wondrous black-and-white masterpieces that could transport him to worlds where evil villains were defeated and beautiful vixens always made the right choice for a true hero. He spent every cent he had on comics and had milk crates full of the epic tales stashed in the garage and hidden in his room. His mother didn't approve of his choice of reading material nor spending money on that choice. Thoughtful son that he was, he protected her by making sure she never found his library.

Further down the hall, Robert spied the Queen of the Loners. She was known as Crazy Charlie Donnelly and she lived in infamy among anyone who had to deal with her. Her real name was Charlene, which didn't suit her as much. Still, if you knew what was good for you, *Charlene* was what you called her. That girl liked to fight.

She was certifiable. Take, for instance, the way she got around town. Every normal kid in the world rode a bicycle; that was the way it was done. But Crazy Charlie *ran*. She ran everywhere, which explained why she was built like a beanpole. And if you asked her why, she'd cut you down with, "Because I like it. Now butt out of my business, pal!" To top it off, she wore men's pants all the time. No decent girl wore men's pants, much less the kind labourers wore, made of blue denim.

He watched as the skinny blond pushed past a group of jocks blocking her path to the water fountain. Charlie was tall and athletic, but they were big and dumb, plus there were four of them. Not odds Robert would have taken on, but then he wasn't nuts.

"Look who's back," the guy built like a bull buffalo sneered. "Dang, Charlie. I see you ain't filled out any more over the summer. I guess I won't be asking you to the prom. Flat as you are, I might mistake you for one of the boys." This drew guffaws and a round of crude comments from his buddies.

Charlie pushed past him. "Out of my way, meathead. I'd punch you but I don't want to chance popping that disgusting and, I might add, *giant* zit on your chin."

Robert had to agree. The pimple was mammoth.

The jock reflexively covered his inflamed sore and angrily reached out to stop her with his other hand. But Charlie was too fast. With a quick elbow jab to his solar plexus, she winded the big goon, then continued to the fountain like nothing had happened.

Robert would have stuck around, but he didn't want to see the dope cry. That was how it always ended when you messed with Crazy Charlie.

EVERY DAY, ROBERT brought his meteorite with him to school. He could reach into his pocket, hold it in his fist and feel its power any time he wanted. He checked it frequently, inspecting the heat-scarred surface and feeling the odd heft of it as it nestled in his palm. He couldn't get over his luck at being there the very moment the meteorite had struck.

The long week lumbered on relentlessly. Finally Friday arrived and Robert burst out of the prison doors, leapt on his bike and screamed down the street toward one of his favourite destinations – Kreller's Drugstore.

As he walked in, a small bell jangled over the door, the same bell that had been there for as long as Robert could remember. He went to the counter and found the pharmacist counting pills and pouring them into a brown glass bottle. He waited politely, taking in the familiar drugstore smells and eyeing the orderly shelves filled with paraphernalia for assorted aches and pains. On the hospital-green walls, colourful posters advertised liniments, stomach remedies and blood tonics guaranteed to make a new man out of you, whether you wanted to be a new man or not. Behind the counter, Mr. Kreller had tacked up his standard signs – no reading magazines for free, no sampling candy for free – and a poster with information on war savings stamps (definitely no getting those for free).

Finally the elderly pharmacist screwed the cap on the bottle and set it aside.

"Hi, Mr. Kreller." Robert piped up before the druggist could start another prescription. He was polite, not patient.

"Well now, there's the laddie I've been waiting for."

Robert's heart sped up a beat. "Someone came in today?" He always referred to the comic books as if they were the hero they contained. To him, it was more natural.

"One of your favourites, *Captain Ice.*" Mr. Kreller walked to the cash register and pulled a brown paper bag from under the counter.

Robert put his quarter down. "He's going home with me." Good thing he'd come in. Mr. Kreller only got one of each title. What if some other kid had beaten him to it?

Mr. Kreller peered over the rims of his half-spectacles and gave Robert a meaningful look. "Supply is tight in these tough times."

No kidding. His mother constantly reminded him it was 1943 and there was a war on so he should be careful – with his clothes, with his bike tires, with his allowance. "Money doesn't grow on trees, don-cha-know." Robert did know, better than anyone. With his fifteen cents change tucked safely in his pocket, he cycled home, his mind turning over his constant problem. Although he tried not to, somehow he always ended up spending every cent of his allowance on comics. The thing was, at ten cents each and with his allowance only a quarter, his favourite three required more money than he usually had at one crack. Sometimes he'd get a few extra cents from his mum, and he got money for his birthday and Christmas, which helped. The problem was saving for his favourites when there were so many others calling his name – *Iron Man, Nelvana of the Northern Lights, Johnny Canuck* and the new guy, *Canada Jack.*

Still, it was easier keeping up now than it had been before the war had started. *Superman, Captain Marvel, Flash Gordon* – in fact, any comics printed in the United States – no longer came to Canada. The War Exchange Conservation Act prevented non-essential goods, like comic books, from coming across the border. Robert would have made a petition and sent it to Prime Minister Mackenzie King if he could have found other kids as crazy about comics as him. It was a good thing his own Canadian superheroes had stepped in or he'd have nothing to read.

Robert peeled around a corner and barely had time to screech on his brakes as a girl leapt out in front of him, crossing the intersection against the light. "Wham! Kablam!" he yelled as he barely avoided running smack into her.

Robert recognized the jaywalker – or jayrunner, rather. It was Crazy Charlie Donnelly. If anyone would break the rules, it would be her.

She scowled at him over her shoulder and he returned the look before she disappeared around a corner. She wasn't going to ruin his good mood. He was too excited to get home and jump into Captain Ice's latest adventure.

Quietly, he slipped in the back door of his house, hoping his mother would not hear and press-gang him into some disgusting chore. He wanted to read his new comic right away.

"Is that you Robert?" his mother called from deep inside the hall closet.

So much for his silent entrance. He swore his mother could hear a pin drop in Berlin. "Who else would it be Mum? Mussolini?"

Robert's mother walked into the kitchen pulling an apron over her head. She was a slim woman, small and strong for her size. She was also one of the most energetic people he knew.

"Enough of your cheek, young man. Why are you so late? I have my Knit for Victory group tonight and need to get supper early. Also, I noticed your shoes are looking terribly scuffed. I know you polish them Saturday night but with this war on and having to make them last, you need to put a little more effort and elbow grease into..."

But Robert wasn't in the kitchen anymore. In his mind, he was far away, on a dangerous mission.

When he first started reading comic books, he'd discovered something amazing. He found that if he concentrated, he could escape into their black-and-white universe and make the real world disappear...

CLOUDS HAD GATHERED AROUND HIM AND THE SCREAM
OF AN ENGINE FILLED HIS MIND. A HAIL OF BULLETS
STREAKED TOWARD OUR UNSUSPECTING HERO IN HIS
LITTLE FIGHTER. THE ENEMY PLANE HAD BEEN HIDING
IN A CLOUD BANK! WITH LIGHTNING SPEED, OUR HERO
DODGED THE ATTACK, THEN USED THE SAME CLOUDS
TO ESCAPE AS HE FLEW INTO THE DENSE MIST
AND DISAPPEARED.

"Robert! I said a letter from George arrived for you. I put it on your desk."

His mother's words yanked Robert back from his imagined world with a jolt. "Really? That's great. Thanks, Mum!" What a lucky day – Captain Ice *and* a letter from his brother!

He raced up the stairs, his long legs taking them two at a time. Depositing the bag with his precious comic on the bed, he picked up the letter. It was battered and marked up, with George's unmistakable scratchy writing scrawled across the envelope.

Robert stood in front of his desk, considering his options. Which one should he read first, Ice's adventure or George's letter?

He had all his brothers' pictures lined up for inspection and their happy faces never failed to lift his spirits. Their family was all boys. George was the oldest, then James, followed by Patrick. Then Robert had shown up. He'd always felt like a late arrival at the party.

In his picture, George stood proudly in front of his Spitfire. His letters were filled with stories of his wild exploits in the air and the close bond he shared with the other pilots. Always a bit of a daredevil, he'd flown escort with the No. 6 Bomber Group. Now he harried the enemy out of an aerodrome in England called Tangmere. Even the name sounded exotic.

Next was James, the playful one. He was in England too, at Portslade, Sussex with the Calgary Highlanders, training the Home Guard to protect Great Britain should the country be invaded. James joked they could only defend the place if the enemy attackers were also over sixty years old and carrying

World War I guns with five rounds of ammunition.

Of all his brothers, Robert was closest to Patrick. They were more than brothers; they were true friends. They'd always stuck up for one another against every foe, especially their mother, who kept a tight rein on her boys. Patrick was fighting in the Mediterranean and commanded his own squad of men.

The four brothers had developed a secret code for writing to one another, in case their letters were intercepted by an enemy spy – foreign or domestic. They also avoided alarming not only those dratted censors but their dear mother, who always wanted to know what her boys were up to. Decoding was complicated and if George had used their cypher, it would take a while to figure it out, perhaps a long while. It made perfect sense to read the comic first.

"Ice it is!" Robert declared aloud. He replaced the envelope on his desk next to George's frame, saluted each picture, then leapt onto his bed.

He took the meteorite out of his pocket and sat it on the bedside table where he could see it. He loved the way the light glinted off the small stone. At that moment, the warm breeze coming through the window stirred his mobile of Allied fighter planes, silently flying them around their tiny sky. He'd made the models when George had enlisted in the Royal Canadian Air Force.

"I'll get to your letter later!" he promised his brother, wherever he was. Eagerly, Robert reached for the paper bag and pulled out the comic.

The cover practically glowed, the colours dazzlingly brilliant, mesmerizing. Robert took in the rugged face of that ace fighter pilot Captain Ice and was immediately transported into his realm of adventure. Ice, in his brown leather bomber jacket and flying cap with goggles, could shoot five enemy planes out of the sky, destroy three ammo factories and then go on to wine and dine some lovely, lonely French Resistance mademoiselle – and still be at the aerodrome bright and early the next morning. Talk about your one-man air force!

The hero was pictured in his fighter plane, *Invincible*, fending off three Focke-Wulf FW 190s, while what looked like stars streamed by the cockpit. His teeth were bared and big beads of sweat gleamed on his brow. As Robert opened the cover and started to read, he was confident his hero would again beat the Nazi scourge. How could he not? The guy was incredible!

Near the end, the story got wildly exciting. One large panel showed Ice about to be blown out of the sky as shooting stars – meteorites! – streaked by like cosmic rain; then, with a blinding flash, a large meteorite shot past the planes, temporarily blinding the enemy pilot. Seizing the opportunity, Ice made his escape by climbing so steeply he nearly stalled his one-of-a-kind super fighter plane. Forcing *Invincible* into a steep dive, the air ace skimmed the treetops before demolishing the train loaded with enemy supplies. The carnage was well drawn, and Robert traced the progress of tanks, freight cars, assorted villains and big chunks of the trestle bridge, as everything fell into a bottomless gorge. He jumped to the last panel where Ice soared home to fight another day.

Robert closed the cover feeling very satisfied, then opened it again and reread the part about the meteorite storm. What a co-incidence that this story had come out so close to him finding his own fallen star.

Grabbing his meteorite, he went downstairs to help with supper.

Later that night, after his torturous homework was done, Robert sat at his desk, placed his meteorite on the worn wooden surface and unfolded George's letter. Sure enough, there was decoding to do, though thankfully not much. Robert finished quickly.

George and his little Spitfire were like a thorn in the side of the Luftwaffe, flying over France, protecting Allied planes and shooting down enemy fighters. In disjointed code, since George wasn't as adept as James and Patrick, he relayed how he'd had a near miss when avoiding an enemy fighter. He'd used a dicey maneuver, requiring a precipitously steep climb, and then a dive back down so fast the G-force nearly made him black out.

He signed off with "Give my love to Mother and don't make her worry." This was a subtle reminder to Robert not to tell their mum anything about the dangerous stuff. The part about avoiding the enemy plane had been exciting...and oddly familiar.

Robert checked his bedside table, where the latest installment of Captain Ice waited for rereading. He retrieved the comic book and skimmed the last part of the story where Ice had to climb steeply and then force the plane into a dangerous dive. Another coincidence! George and Ice, Robert's two favourite pilots, both had to execute a crazy maneuver to escape a close call.

He examined the cover, the way it depicted the meteorite storm streaming past *Invincible* as Ice fought his enemies. Reaching for his own little star, Robert held the fragment in his palm, once again feeling the odd sensation of warmth. He closed his fist protectively around his treasure.

Weird or what?

CHAPTER THREE

LUCKY NEIGHBOURS

OVER THE WEEKEND, Robert spent his free time reading comic books and inspecting his meteorite. The small wonder fascinated him. What luck to have been out exploring at exactly the right spot at exactly the right moment his special delivery arrived – for that was how he thought of it, as a present from the universe, a prize for braving the night alone. It was dull grey and metallic, like molten metal frozen into a perfect little planet he could hold. Sitting in his room, he memorized every fold and crevasse on the pebble. He traced the smooth surfaces and probed the tiny canyons.

Monday after school, Robert again stopped by the drugstore and was rewarded with the latest copy of *Sedna of the Sea*, the second of his favourites. Sedna, like that Canadian icon, *Nelvana of the Northern Lights*, was from the frozen Arctic. Both these fighting females were worthy of the title Comic Book Queen. Nelvana's gifts were extraordinary. She could ride on a giant beam of aurora borealis light, and make herself invisible. Still, it was Sedna of the Sea, in her ocean-blue and sea foam-green suit with a flowing cape, who had the absolute best super powers. Sedna, with her iconic symbol of narwhales with crossed tusks emblazoned on her chest, commanded all the animals in the sea and could travel along pathways of ice she created in ocean currents. Plus she could make time slow or speed up. Robert thought being able to speed up time would be very useful, especially when he was sitting in a particularly boring class.

Mr. Kreller slid the paper bag with the comic in it across the counter. Robert took it, feeling like a secret agent taking a hand-off from a foreign spy.

"I have a copy of *Johnny Canuck* if you're interested," Mr. Kreller offered.

Robert shook his head. "No thanks. I'm hoping the Maple Leaf Kid will come in tomorrow, and my set will be complete for this month." He relinquished a dime for the comic. He had one nickel left to his name, not enough to buy the Kid if he did come in. It was a good thing tomorrow was allowance day. With only a single copy of his absolute favourite hero's adventure due to arrive, he *had* to be the one to scoop it up.

The Kid was a hero anyone could relate to – only sixteen, incredibly smart, truly brave and a patriotic Canadian. Whatever he wore – school blazer, sweater or jacket – there was always a red maple leaf symbol on the breast pocket. He travelled with his father who worked for military intelligence, and solved mysteries, foiled plots and saved the free world through his brilliant use of observation and deduction. The Kid had no super powers. To Robert, this made him seem real, like a next-door neighbour or something. And the way he looked...well, according to the letters printed in the fan section, people thought the Kid was clean cut and boyishly handsome, a great example of an ideal Canadian teenager. Robert liked that a lot because the cartoonist had drawn the Kid with dark hair and brown eyes, a rather prominent nose, a lanky build and an uncanny resemblance to...a certain Robert Tourond!

"Yes, another delivery day tomorrow. I'll have the copy waiting – as long as you think you'll still be interested..." The pharmacist waited.

"No fear there, Mr. Kreller. I'm the Kid's biggest fan and I know he'd be disappointed if I didn't tag along to keep him company on his adventures." He grabbed the bag containing his precious copy of *Sedna of the Sea* and left the store.

IT WAS A SPECTACULAR fall day and the air glowed with that warm golden light you only get in the autumn. Knowing his mother would find work for him the minute he got home, Robert opted to sit in the shade of a poplar with brilliant yellow leaves and read his newest acquisition.

As soon as Robert pulled the comic out, he was riveted by the brightly coloured scene on the cover. Sedna and her ocean creatures were dragging seaweed nets through an icy fjord where the Nazis had hidden a submarine. Moonlight shone on their nets, which were filled with deadly mines.

He flipped the comic open and began to read. The powerful sub could fire self-guided rockets underwater to destroy Allied ships many miles away. Sedna had to stop the sub or hundreds, perhaps thousands, of our boys would be killed. As the submarine readied for launch, Sedna and her swimming commandoes stealthily tangled the mine-filled nets around the propellers. When the Nazis started the engines, the sub – and the scientists who designed it – would be blown to shrapnel. Simple and effective.

Sedna was about to send a special signal to warn her sea creatures to clear the area. Eager to find out what would happen next, Robert turned the page. His breath caught. The signal Sedna was using was *a falling star hitting the ocean.* A meteorite!

He thought of the latest Captain Ice adventure. In all the years he'd been reading comics, he'd never seen shooting stars used in the story. Now here were two. He touched the pebble in his shirt pocket and felt its warmth pulsing. What were the odds of that happening?

WHEN HE ARRIVED HOME there was a bag of trash waiting by the kitchen door, his mother's not-so-subtle way of reminding him he'd forgotten to take it out. He missed having his brothers to share the load. That and to toss a ball around with. His father worked at a fertilizer factory and had to go on shift at five in the morning. He often had to work overtime too, making him so tired all the time that he never played hockey or football with Robert.

Robert dumped his school satchel, then hefted the bag and walked out back to the burn barrel. He tossed the garbage into the old oil drum, then set it afire. Across the alley his neighbour was working in his small appliance repair shop, which used to be his garage. He was a heavyset man with iron-grey hair and he kept to himself mostly, grunting greetings in Polish. His English was sometimes hard to understand, but he and Robert managed all right.

"Hey, Mr. G!" Robert wiped his fingers on his pants and walked over. "What's new in the land of toasters?"

The G was short for Glowinski, a name difficult for Robert to pronounce correctly. His neighbour was a genius with anything electric – there wasn't a radio or Mixmaster on the planet he couldn't fix. Mr. G was an electrical engineer by trade and worked in an office downtown, but he also fixed small appliances in his spare time. Robert suspected he liked being a repairman best.

"I think nothing new under sun, Robcio, not this pressing machine, that is for sure." He picked up the newly repaired clothes iron and plugged it in. "Now, we see if done correctly."

They both waited expectantly. After a couple of minutes, they were rewarded with a noisy *whoosh* of steam.

"*Powodzenia!*" Robert cheered. It meant "good luck" and was his favourite Polish word of the few he'd learned. He particularly liked the "pow" part.

"*Tak, tak,* yes, yes, we have *sukces!*" Mr. G saw the confusion on Robert's face and clarified. "Same as English, success. Good job." He unplugged the iron to let it cool. "So what young man like you up to?"

"School's back in and, from what I can tell, it hasn't improved since last year."

"That good. Stay in school. Make best future for you. Now, you tell me what news."

Robert thought of his extraordinary find, then rummaged in his pocket. "Actually, something pretty strange did happen. I was on Nose Hill and saw this fall from the sky." Excitedly, he showed his neighbour the treasure. "It's an honest-to-goodness meteorite. I think this is killer-diller."

Mr. G's face darkened. "*Killer-diller* not good English. You should not say *killer* anything. *Diller*, okay." Taking the fragment from Robert, he examined it. "Very interesting. I think this one mostly iron."

"It's part of a star that blew up millions of years ago. I'm sure of it."

"Perhaps," Mr. G rolled the pebble around. "You should take care of this, Robcio. Do research at library. Find out about your fallen star."

A crazy idea popped into Robert's head and he knew without a doubt it was the right thing. "Say, is there any way you could make it into something...something I could wear around my neck, you know, for like, *powodzenia?* Please?"

The big man shrugged. "Anything is possible. Now it is quiet time for fix it shop. I see what I can do."

"Gosh, that would be big-time swell!" Robert felt his face flush. He sounded like a little kid. "I mean, thanks Mr. G." Lucky thing Mr. G had the time right now, and a *really* lucky thing he was willing to help out. The idea of leaving the meteorite behind gave Robert a momentary flash of panic but he knew it would be worth it if he could always have the fantastic stone next to his heart.

CHAPTER FOUR

END OF LIFE AS HE KNEW IT

THE NEXT MORNING, Robert awoke eagerly. With luck, today would be Maple Leaf Kid Day, the most exciting day of the month. And with only a nickel left from his previous comic book shopping, he was glad today was also allowance day. His mother paid him on Tuesdays because she said she didn't have time on the weekend, her busiest volunteering days. She needed Monday to figure out if he should have any of his precious twenty-five cents docked for some sin he'd committed. After school he'd shoot by the drugstore and pick up his friend.

He was enjoying breakfast when, without warning, the lucky streak Robert had been enjoying screeched to a halt. His mother stormed into the kitchen, holding his torn pants in front of her like a dead animal. The oatmeal spoon halted halfway to Robert's mouth.

When the last of his brothers had left to fight overseas, Robert began to notice he'd catch Holy Hannah from his mother over the littlest things. He'd decided it was either because she was worried about her soldier sons or she needed someone to blast on a regular basis and he was the only target within range. He felt like he had a bullseye on the back of every shirt. So he'd buried the pants in his closet after that wondrous night he'd found the meteorite and then forgotten about them. He was in for it now. Robert returned the spoon to the bowl and waited, wishing he could run for the nearest foxhole.

"Robert! It's 1943 and there's a war on! You know perfectly well every extra cent we have goes to buying Victory Bonds to help your brothers fight *that Hitler.* Your father and I try very hard to make a good home for you during these terrible times. You have no idea how difficult this is, what with the rationing and all. There is certainly no money left over to keep you in new clothes every week..."

CAUGHT OFF GUARD, OUR BRAVE HERO HEARD THE ENEMY PLANE REV UP ITS ENGINES AND KNEW HE WAS IN MORTAL DANGER. HE SHOULD RUN! HE SHOULD HIDE! BUT ESCAPE WAS IMPOSSIBLE!

"...Robert. Robert!" Robert flinched as he was abruptly yanked back to the real world. His mother was shaking the pants at him now. "I said, what on earth happened to these trousers?"

"Not so much what on earth, Mum, as what hit the earth," he hastily explained. "I was on Nose Hill and saw a shooting star. It fell close to where I was, and you're not going to believe this...I found it! I found a real meteorite! I guess my pants got a little snagged in the hunt."

"You went to Nose Hill...*alone...at night?*"

Too late, he realized his error.

HE WATCHED HELPLESSLY AS HIS FOE'S PLANE SCREAMED INTO THE AIR LIKE A SHARK DRAWN BY THE SCENT OF BLOOD. DEFENCES LIMITED, OUR HERO BRAVELY SCRAMBLED TO SAVE HIMSELF AND HIS LITTLE FIGHTER.

"Uh, it wasn't really night, more late, *late* afternoon, really,"

"Robert, what if something had happened to you? No one would know until they found your bones! And what a worry it would be for your father and me. Every day, wondering where our boy was, hoping you hadn't been taken like that poor little

Lindberg baby, fearing the worst..."

He had to stop this avalanche of unwarranted concern. "There's nothing to worry about Mum. I can take care of myself and I don't think there's ever been a kidnapping in Calgary." He tried to lighten the mood with humour. "Besides, kidnappers take rich people's kids for ransom and that sure ain't us."

His mother stiffened and the unwarranted concern changed to indignant anger. Robert realized he'd made another serious tactical mistake.

ENGINE DAMAGED, OUR HERO KNEW HE COULDN'T OUTRUN THE DEADLY ASSAULT. HE'D HAVE TO USE ALL HIS EXPERT SKILL IF HE WAS GOING TO SHAKE THE ENEMY OFF HIS TAIL. VALIANTLY, HE FLEW ON THROUGH THE STORM!

"Uh, I mean, I'm sure we have enough loot that any kidnapper would love to snatch me up."

"Stop your impertinence young man. We may not be rich but you never go hungry and we live an honest, decent life! And speaking of not being rich, when I found your pants balled up like a chore rag..." Her glare pinned him like a butterfly to a board. "I also found a stack of those blasted comic books. There must be over five dollars worth! Considering how hard your father works to put food on the table, spending money on something so frivolous is completely wrong. Practically *sinful*." Here she made the sign of the cross.

When his mother brought religion into it, Robert knew he was done for. If she found the boxes hidden in the garage, she'd organize a firing squad and borrow the bullets! Or worse – donate his precious collection to a paper drive for the war effort!

WITH A SINKING FEELING, OUR HERO REALIZED HIS AERIAL ACROBATICS WERE NOT ENOUGH TO WIN THIS DISMAL DOGFIGHT. THE ODDS WERE STACKED AGAINST HIM AND HE HOPED HIS PARACHUTE WOULD OPEN....

Robert tried to steer the conversation back to safer ground. "I read those comics over and over, Mum. I get my money's worth out of them." Reading his comics several times was kind of like giving himself a hand-me-down, which he knew his mother was all for. "And they tell fantastic stories about fighting the evil Axis – especially *that Hitler*." He referred to the leader of the Axis powers the way his mother always did, as if the man were something nasty on the bottom of a shoe, to help make his point. "They really boost my morale and make me want to help the war effort in any way I can." Maybe adding this patriotic sentiment would also help his case.

"Nevertheless, it's a lot of money. This is about growing up as much as anything Robert. In fact, I think it's high time you discovered what it takes to make those dimes you so freely squander on your funny papers."

"They're not funny papers Mum, those are in the newspapers. They're comic books and they're important and worth every penny of my hard-earned allowance."

His mother's face grew pinched. "Is that so, Robert Joseph Tourond?"

Robert sucked in his breath. The triple-barrelled name thing was a sure sign he was a goner.

TIME STOPPED AS OUR HERO DESPERATELY BANKED HIS BATTERED LITTLE FIGHTER. THE ENEMY HELD THE SUPERIOR POSITION AND STARTED A DEADLY STRAFING RUN HE COULD NOT ESCAPE.

"Your 'hard-earned allowance'," she scoffed. "Maybe I should get paid for washing your clothes or cooking your meals!"

Robert knew what sarcasm was. He'd taken it in English. He kept quiet.

"Does your father ask for payment from you when he gets up at four o'clock every day and goes to the factory so you can eat?"

THE DOGFIGHT HAD TURNED INTO THE BATTLE OF HIS LIFE!

"And next time your trousers need mending because you were careless while gallivanting around hell's half acre, I'll show you where the sewing box is and you can fix them yourself!"

Understanding dawned like a 60-watt light bulb going on. Mum must have had a letter from George. Even with the censors cutting out most of the good stuff, hearing about his exploits always made her a little strange.

"Mum, maybe I should make you a nice cup of tea. We could both use a cup of really, *really* strong tea, and the sooner the better, I say...."

His mother scrutinized the ruined pants – a hanging judge examining the bloody evidence. Tension grew while Robert waited for the verdict. She straightened. "You shall still receive your allowance...."

Wham! Kablam! He'd truly dodged a bullet this time. Robert relaxed – but too soon, it turned out.

"However, from now on," she continued, cranking up the meat grinder to "pulverize", "the entire amount will go toward buying war savings certificates which will support your brothers who are fighting so hard to keep the world free from *that Hitler.*"

As Robert digested the words, his satisfaction fizzled to be replaced with anger.

BLEEDING AND NEARLY OUT OF AMMO, OUR BRAVE HERO WOULDN'T GO DOWN WITHOUT A FIGHT, NO MATTER HOW FUTILE HIS DYING EFFORTS. HE RELOADED HIS GUNS WITH THE LAST OF HIS BULLETS.

"That's not fair Mum! I earn that money doing chores around the house. It's mine. I should get to spend it on anything I like."

For once, she ignored his rude tone. "This is a life lesson. Growing up successfully is all about responsibility and making wise choices. I believe this is a very good start for you."

WITH THE FINAL SALVO DELIVERED DIRECTLY ON TARGET, THE ENEMY WHIRLED IN A VICTORY ROLL AND DEPARTED AS OUR HERO'S LITTLE FIGHTER SPIRALLED DOWN IN FLAMES. IS THIS THE END?

His mother stalked out of the room like a conquering general leaving the bloody field of battle. Robert stood speechless, knowing it was useless to protest. They'd had the "responsibility" conversation before, but the part about his allowance going to buy war savings certificates was completely new. His mother was all for the war effort. Heck, hadn't she'd ripped up her precious flowerbed to plant a victory garden? But now she was volunteering *him* to be part of her master plan to defeat the Nazis!

Rationing didn't affect him. Less gasoline meant nothing – his family didn't have a car. It was his mother who made do with the weekly allotments of a half-pound of butter and eight ounces of sugar, and since they were Catholic, they didn't eat meat on Fridays anyway, so the required "meatless day" was covered. Robert didn't mind using less natural gas for heat – he wore undershirts and sweaters in winter.

But doing without the money that kept him in comic books – he felt like he'd been kicked in the gut. The idea of a world without comic books was unthinkable and, for him, unlivable.

Then he remembered. *The Maple Leaf Kid* was due in today and he had only one measly nickel left. This was a disaster! His brain frantically sought a solution. Maybe she'd calm down by tonight and it would all blow over?

Trying to control himself, Robert grabbed his school bag and was about to slam out the door when his mother came back into the kitchen.

"Robert, good, you're still here. You received this from James." She held an envelope out to him, her face as calm as the eye of a hurricane. "It slipped my mind. I got my own letter from your foolhardy brother George. Then I found your new pants, and well, I guess it was the straw that broke the camel's back." She rubbed her forehead wearily, like she had a headache. "Oh, and about your allowance, I shouldn't have been so angry..."

Immediately hopeful, Robert tucked his letter in his book bag and waited respectfully, altar-boy perfect, sure she'd come to her senses.

"...but it really is for your own good dear. You'll thank me when you cash in your certificates and there's all that added interest."

The shell with his name on it exploded. Yes, he'd thank her – in seven and a half years when the certificates came due! It was forever away and there wasn't a darn thing he could do. Once his mother made her mind up, no power in any universe could change the course of that juggernaut. His voice broke as he replied. "I'm sure I will, Mum."

There would be tough words in his next letter to his eldest brother. He knew it had been George's bragging that had sent her down this motherly path of destruction.

WHEELING HIS BIKE dejectedly out of the garage, Robert was at a loss as to what to do. Comics were his life; but money was required to keep the lifeblood flowing. Money was supposed to be the root of all evil. If that was the case, he could sure use a piece of that root. He'd plant it and pray for rain.

His gloomy thoughts were interrupted by Mr. Glowinski.

"Robcio! You have minute?"

"Sure Mr. G, what's up?" He pushed his bike to his neighbour's garage.

"I work on meteorite last night. It is finished. It turn out pretty good. You want to see?"

Immediately Robert's spirits lifted. "It's done! So soon? I mean, it's ready now?" He laid his bike down gently, careful not to scratch it. "You bet I want to see!" His heart sped up. Today was supposed to be his favourite day of the month, *Maple Leaf Kid Day*, but it had been blown up with his mother's unbelievable tirade. The return of his meteorite would put one thing right at least.

They walked into the cool garage and went to the workbench. Hanging from an ancient drill press was his fallen star. Mr. G had worked the stone to shape it, showing off the intricate detail on a surface etched by millions of years of interstellar travel. He'd tunnelled into the rock and attached an ornate loop of gold metal through which passed a gleaming silver chain.

Robert was mesmerized, unable to speak. "Wham...Kablam..." he finally whispered as he watched the light reflect off the small work of art. "This is too much Mr. G!"

The big man waved dismissively. "It is nothing. Good to work on something that does not need electricity."

"It's beautiful, and the fancy chain...I was going to use a piece of string."

"Use binder twine on my beautiful work! *Nie, nie.* I had chain and it was right tool for job." He lifted the necklace off the press and gave it to Robert.

The talisman nestled in Robert's palm. It still had that strange, otherworldly warmth, and as he slipped the chain over his head, he had the odd sensation it was humming. He was sure the stone was happy; it was where it belonged, home from its uncharted wanderings at last.

There was another Polish word Robert knew and though he couldn't pronounce it correctly, he gave it his best shot. "*Dziękuję.*" He tried not to show the sudden wave of emotion he felt. "Thank you."

"Humph," Mr. G replied as he busily gathered his screwdrivers and pliers from the bench then put them away in his tool box and snapped the lid closed. "Now I must be engineer for government. Go to school, get education so you can have good job, like me." He shooed Robert away in dismissal.

Robert touched the stone and felt a tingle. He would keep this gift from the universe with him always.

CHAPTER FIVE

FAT CHANCE

ROBERT DECIDED TO KEEP his treasure hidden beneath his shirt at school as none of his swell-headed classmates would understand how important it was. They already called him Comic Book Crazy and he didn't want to add Buck Rogers Space Cadet to their list of uncomplimentary nicknames. As he wended his way down the hallway he could feel the stone's warmth against his skin and was glad he'd brought it.

Miss Pettigrew, his homeroom teacher, was pinning a poster to the wall when he entered his classroom. Her hair was piled haphazardly on top of her head – a style Robert thought of as Haystack Madness – and she always smelled faintly of old cigarettes and stale perfume. Miss Pettigrew was what his parents would have called "eccentric."

"Boys and girls, to start the school year off right we're going to have a grand contest open to all students!" she announced, pushing in the last thumbtack. "It's the cat's meow!"

Robert scanned the poster. The contest was called The Great Grease Roundup. The student who collected the most fat over the next two weeks would win a full book of twenty-five-cent war savings stamps.

"Wham. Kablam," he murmured as he reread the poster. Those stamps were as good as money. In fact, the poster on the wall of Mr. Kreller's drugstore, the one about the war stamps, advertised how he would give savings stamps in lieu of change. An idea flashed into Robert's mind. What if Mr. Kreller would do it the other way around and *take* savings stamps in lieu of money? A full book was worth four whole dollars. If Robert could convince the old pharmacist to do a trade, he would be rolling in comic books for a long, l-o-n-g time.

He was getting ahead of himself. First, he had to win this contest.

It was then he noticed someone else eyeing the poster with interest. It was Crazy Charlie Donnelly: trouble with a blond ponytail. If Robert was going to take the prize, he had to eliminate the competition. He made his way over. "Planning on entering?" he asked casually.

"Maybe," she answered, in the same bland tone.

"Seems like a lot of trouble for a few stamps." Robert trod carefully, trying not to alert her to how much he wanted to win.

"Yeah, the thing is, I'm kinda bored right now and it would give me something to do after school. Wonder if it matters what kind of fat?"

Robert thought this was an odd thing to say. In addition to all her other faults, Charlie must be a little slow, as his mother would say. Time to educate the poor thing. "I think it means ordinary fat, you know, like grease from bacon. It's used to make glycerine, which they need to manufacture nitroglycerine which is used in explosives, like bombs..."

Her lips compressed into a thin line, like she was biting back a bullet or two herself. "I was talking about animal or vegetable, genius, and if it has to be fresh. What about shelf life or expiry dates?" The look she gave him made his ego shrink five sizes. He hadn't thought about any of that. "Then," she went on, "I decided since it's going to be processed, maybe the condition wouldn't matter much. However, my Uncle Gus, he's a chef at a restaurant, says you have to be careful with fat because it goes rancid."

"Rancid?"

Now Charlie looked at him like he was the slow one. "Rotten."

"Oh yeah, I forgot," he lied, none too smoothly.

She crossed her arms. "If it doesn't have to be in good shape, then there's a lot more out there for me to collect."

Robert saw where she was going. "I think it would be against the rules to get it from your uncle's restaurant. That would give you an unfair advantage, Charlie...."

The second he let her nickname slip, he knew he'd made a mistake. She whirled on him, criminal acts in her eyes and poisonous venom on her lips.

"Oh yeah? Why don't you show old *Crazy Charlie* where it says I can't tap into family resources?" Her acid tone could have stripped the paint off a battleship.

She jerked her thumb at the poster and Robert had to admit there was nothing there about where the fat should come from. He saw his war stamps floating away on a sea of grease. "Fine. You need to remember one small detail – two can play at that game Char*lene!*"

A crowd of kids had gathered, elbowing one another as they tried to get closer to what they hoped would turn into a knock-down, drag-out battle. From the comments, he knew for once the mob was on his side. A lock of Robert's unruly black hair fell forward over one eye and he brushed it back with annoyance. Would he have to actually hit her? His mother would shoot him and his father would hand her the gun.

"Ladies and gentlemen!" Miss Pettigrew clapped loudly to get everyone's attention. "Take your seats please! It doesn't matter where the grease comes from. We need to keep in mind this is for an extremely important cause. Bring your contribution to the home economics room each morning and I will weigh it and add the amount to your total. The winner will be announced at Friday assembly in two weeks' time."

As the crowd dispersed, Charlie glared at Robert and he tried to eyeball her back with equal intensity. Sadly, his attempt to shoot daggers failed. He was more of a butter-knife man.

CHAPTER SIX

_____

A BIG HAIRY SACRIFICE

AS ROBERT SAT THROUGH the most mind-numbing classes on the planet, he worried about getting his comic books and what he would do if he didn't win the fat contest. Winning those savings stamps was his best shot at long-term money. Then there was his immediate battle: getting that *Maple Leaf Kid.* Robert knew Mr. Kreller wouldn't sell it to him for just his lone nickel.

He had no choice. He'd have to use the only piece of ammo he had, even if it was like fixing a leaking dam by jamming chewing gum in the crack. It would be hard to bear but he'd do it. No way would he abandon the Kid.

AS SOON AS SCHOOL let out, Robert climbed on his bike and, gritting his teeth, headed down to Sixth Avenue. His mother had given him money for his back-to-school haircut. He used to go to the neighbourhood barber, Mr. Bert. Then he discovered the Marvel Beauty Academy and Scientific Hairdressing Salon. It was a school for hairdressers. Its claim to fame: you could get a really cheap cut if you were willing to gamble on the competence of the students. Last time the cut had ended up pretty odd, with one side a lot shorter than the other, and his mum had said she was going to have a word with Mr. Bert.

Fortunately she hadn't. Robert had vowed not to chance it again, but he was desperate. He thought of the five cents he would save as danger pay, so he could add it, guilt-free, to his comic book fund.

Soon Robert sat stiffly in the lady barber's chair. He refused to call her a hairdresser – a guy had to hold on to some pride. To pass the time, he pulled James' letter out of his book bag. He'd been unsuccessfully trying to read it all day. Now he could relax and enjoy a laugh; he knew the letter would have a funny story, in code of course, and it did.

> *Hi-de-ho Robert,*
>
> *Things here are hoppin'. Lots of pretty kittens who'll trade a date for new mittens. Which reminds me, can you ask mum if she'd send over something a girl would like – silk stockings would be swell. I'm a dead hoofer, but with those, the ladies would think I'm king of the local dance club. Rationing is tough. It's been a while since I ate real hen fruit. That powdered heifer dust they serve in the mess ain't like the real deal.*
>
> *Hey, here's something a one-striper like you would enjoy. Last week, my chaps and I followed a swarm of bees to their hive by the river. Can't have the bees stinging my lads so we decided to get rid of the problem. It got exciting, bees being what they are and all. We had to use balls of pine sap to stop those flying pests from stinging. One of the chaps forgot he'd left his best Sunday cap on a ball of sap by a fallen branch and when he went back for it, a strong wind blew everything away! For his trouble, the fellow got a couple of small bee stings, but the cap and branch were gone into the big blue beyond. I had to explain to the fellow's wife about losing the cap and the branch and she said we should have let the bees take them and spared her poor husband the stings! I'll tell you, there was hell to pay and the devil to bribe.*
>
> *Give Dad and Mum my love and don't flap your lips too much. We wouldn't want Mum to blow a gasket like she does with George!*

See you in the funny papers,
James

When Robert had the whole letter translated into a note-book, he read it again, skipping over the boring chatter and getting right to the good stuff. James hadn't let him down.

Hey, here's something a little brother like you would enjoy. Last week my Home Guard Troops and I were sent to the coast to stop enemy ships from infiltrating the harbour. Can't have those devils blowing up anything. We had to be careful of snipers. We set out mines so no enemy ships could sneak in and sabotage. One of the Home Guard accidentally set off a mine by a pier, destroying both. The fellow had minor injuries, which was lucky considering everything was blown to smithereens. I was the one who had to explain to the Captain how we managed to injure a guard and do as much damage as the enemy! I got into a lot of trouble but talked my way out of most of it.

Robert knew James would have used his best talent, that old Tourond silver tongue, to smooth things over with his captain. That was one handy gift he wished he shared with his story telling brother, especially when he had to deal with his mum.

Robert liked the idea of James making things safer for the Brits. They'd been through so much, particularly the Londoners – hiding out in the Underground every night while fire rained down during the Blitz; the total destruction of whole streets of houses; never knowing if a friend or neighbour would be killed in an instant. Their rationing was much worse too. James had told him he couldn't remember the last time he'd seen an orange. It made Canada seem very safe. Robert decided the next time he had a piece of fruit, he'd eat it in James' honour.

His brothers led an exciting life, that was for sure. They were living in a world of danger and daring that rivalled many of Robert's favourite comic book adventures. He would give anything to be over there, fighting alongside them instead of simply reading about their exploits.

It was then he remembered Sedna of the Sea's latest adventure, blowing up a submarine with a net full of mines. Something lit up in the back of Robert's mind...

"Okay sailor, you're done."

The lady barber swirled away his cape, blowing a pink bubble from the gum she'd been snapping the whole time she'd hacked at his hair.

Robert checked the mirror and nearly jumped. It was much shorter than usual, almost a brush cut. He ran his fingers across the bristly stubble. His dad would like the new style. Unfortunately, it meant no more saved haircut money for quite a while.

Stowing James' letter in his bag, Robert hurried to the front desk and paid, safely tucking his hard-earned nickel into the pocket of his trousers.

Now came his reward. It was Maple Leaf Kid time!

Robert raced to Kreller's drugstore. His heart sank as he wheeled up to the store and saw the *Closed* sign in the window. He'd have to wait another day to go on a new adventure with his hero. Then, the unthinkable struck him. What if Mr. Kreller had *sold* the only copy of the Kid to someone else? The fear and disappointment were so sharp he felt a little sick. A familiar figure far down the street caught his eye. Robert pumped the pedals on his bike.

"*Mr. Kreller! Mr. Kreller!*" he called, chasing after the pharmacist. "Wait! *Stop!*"

Mr. Kreller turned. "Robert! My goodness, you gave me quite a start."

"Did *The Maple Leaf Kid* come in today?" Robert asked, a little breathless from his sprint. He dug in his pocket and pulled out the two nickels. "If he did, please can I buy it? I have the money."

"Yes, your comic came in. Now, as you can see, lad, I'm on my way home for supper and the shop's locked up tight. Tell you what, I'll keep it for you. Come by after school tomorrow and you can pick it up then."

A sliver of panic stabbed Robert. *"No!* I mean, *please* Mr. Kreller, couldn't you come back and open the store for me, just this once? I've waited and waited for this issue." This was true. He waited and waited for every issue of *The Maple Leaf Kid.* After all, it was his favourite. "I'd be so grateful. I can't tell you what it would mean to me. I worry so much about my brothers fighting overseas; the only comfort I get is from my comic books." He knew this was laying it on pretty thick, but he saw the hesitation on the old man's face. *"Please* Mr. Kreller."

"All right, all right. I guess this once wouldn't hurt. I think Rosemary is making her casserole delight for dinner and believe me, that's one delight that I can wait for." He turned back toward the darkened store.

Robert walked his bike beside the pharmacist, palms sweating. His pendant suddenly warmed against his skin and he felt the stone thrumming again. This had been too close.

The second he had the brown paper bag he felt miraculously better. "Thank you. You have no idea what this means to me."

The elderly pharmacist nodded wearily in understanding. "I have a grandson fighting over there and I know how it preys on a body's mind."

Robert squeezed the bag tightly. Now was as good a time as any. He took a deep breath. "Ah, sir...I saw your sign about giving trading stamps for change, and I was wondering, if I brought in a full book of stamps...now, we're talking *completely full*...would you give me four dollars store credit toward comic books?"

Mr. Kreller was skeptical. "It's usually the other way around – people buy saving stamps from me. You know that if you trade the book in for a certificate, you'll make a lot more money in the end?"

"Yeah. The thing is, I kinda can't wait that long." Robert had been buying comics from this store since he was high enough to reach the counter and hoped loyalty counted for something. He was desperate and decided it wouldn't hurt to sweeten the pot. "What if I gave you the full book of stamps, four dollars' worth, and you gave me store credit for only *three* dollars? That way you come out *one whole dollar* ahead. And since I would take the credit out in comic books, no cash would actually leave the store."

The shopkeeper chuckled. *"One whole dollar* you say! You must really want this badly. You'd be giving away ten comic books." He considered the offer. "You're a good customer, and I like to take care of my customers. I think we can arrange something – on a *one time only* basis, you understand. The deal is the book must be completely full, and I will give you the entire value, four dollars."

A weight floated off Robert's shoulders and he felt positively giddy. "Oh, it will be, sir. You bet!" He was elated.

While Mr. Kreller relocked the drugstore, Robert leapt on his bike and aimed it for home. The wind whistled over his close-cropped head and he shivered. Today had been a really close shave, literally. He *had* to win the Great Grease Roundup at school. There was no other option. Life would be meaningless without comics.

As he turned down his alley, Robert put his worry aside. After all, he had a new comic book, and not just any comic book. He had the latest edition of *The Maple Leaf Kid!* Was there anything better in the entire universe? And he had a hunch this one would be particularly interesting.

CHAPTER SEVEN

MESSAGE FROM THE UNIVERSE

WHEN ROBERT ARRIVED HOME he rocketed up the stairs, anticipating his new adventure with the Kid. Offering a quick salute to each of his brothers' pictures sitting stoically on his dresser, he jumped onto his bed, arranged his pillows like he was a fearless space explorer blasting off in his ship, and prepared to be dazzled.

With the world's most uncanny sense of timing, his mother chose then to walk into the room, a pair of trousers hanging from her arm. He stifled his immediate groan with a cough; he didn't want to spend two hours scrubbing the latrine with a toothbrush for insubordination to a commanding officer.

WITHOUT WARNING, THE ENEMY PLANE DROPPED INTO OUR HERO'S SKY. HE BANKED HIS LITTLE FIGHTER HARD AS HE FLED FOR COVER. TRAGICALLY, IT WAS TOO LATE. HE'D BEEN SPOTTED.

Then Robert remembered James' letter and knew she was here for every juicy detail.

"James is fine Mum, and sends his love. He wrote how he's been showing the Home Guard some stuff about bees." True enough. She could read the letter herself and learn that very thing. He hoped this would satisfy his mother, who was always snooping for news not included in his brothers' letters to her.

His mother laid the trousers on his bed, smoothing out imaginary creases. "I couldn't let good clothes go to waste and I know how limited *your* sewing skills are. Try not to do any more damage. My ration card couldn't take it."

That was it? He was off the hook. This was too good to be true.

UNEXPECTEDLY, THE ENEMY FLEW BEHIND A JAGGED PEAK AND DISAPPEARED, LEAVING OUR HERO TO BREATHE A SIGH OF RELIEF. HE WAS SAFE FOR ANOTHER DAY, ANOTHER BATTLE.

"Actually, it isn't only the pants I'm here to deliver. You are one lucky boy Robert. You received a letter from Patrick in today's post. I hope mine comes tomorrow since..." here she paused dramatically, "...*I didn't get one.*" She took the letter out of her apron pocket.

Robert was surprised. It was very unusual to get letters from all three of his brothers so close together. Sometimes neither his parents nor he would get anything for weeks and weeks then a single letter would show up, battered and crumpled, relieving at least some of their fear.

He took his letter as his mother walked to the window. "We'd best air the lair. It smells like a grizzly's been hibernating in here."

Robert wondered if she was stalling until he opened his mail. "If you'd like, I'll bring both James and Patrick's letters down later and you can read them after supper, kind of like for dessert."

"I must admit, I'd appreciate a chance to catch up with what they've been up to, dear." She patted him on the shoulder and then turned and left, her mission accomplished.

Robert had to be the luckiest guy in Canada. He had the latest edition of *The Maple Leaf Kid* and a letter from a brother – again! But Patrick was his favourite so he didn't have to think about his choice this time. He tore open the envelope and placed the letter on the bedspread in front of him. His brother's writing, so familiar and reassuring, rambled casually across the page, and Robert knew everything was okay. He decoded his brother's words.

> *Buongiorno, Roberto, as they say here.*
>
> *Things are going well. My guys are all healthy and complaining about the food. I tell them to think of bully beef as fine steak. They say they're having trouble "swallowing" that. Ha Ha.*
>
> *Twenty thousand Canadians are here in Sicily. A couple of days ago we camped on the sides of Mount Etna, an active volcano. Instead of watching the pretty lava flow, we spent our nights in foxholes, dodging snipers, and our days slogging across the rocky terrain. It's been raining a lot and we all smell like wet dogs. I've fought, marched, slept, ate and bathed with my Vickers machine gun. I've grown so attached to the darn thing, maybe I should offer to marry it.*
>
> *We're on the east coast now and Monty is taking us across the Strait of Messina into Italy today. We're expecting heavy fighting. Wish me luck!*
>
> *I miss you, mon frere.*
>
> *Love,*
>
> *Patrick*
>
> *P.S. The wildest thing happened early this morning. It was about five o'clock, I couldn't sleep, nerves I guess, and was staring up at the sky when I saw a shooting star. It was the brightest one I have ever seen; it lit up the night. I followed it from east to west until it disappeared. It was something to write home about, so I did. Ha ha again.*

Robert reread the words, then checked the decoded date: Friday, September 3. If he allowed for the time difference between Sicily and Canada, Patrick had seen his shooting star at the exact time Robert saw his! He touched the stone. Had it been the same one? His had been particularly brilliant too. He remembered the searing light and the blinding afterimage.

Robert shivered and reached for the drugstore bag. *The Maple Leaf Kid* would bring everything back to normal. But when he drew the comic book out, he gasped and clutched at his tiny rock pendant. It felt hot against his chest.

The Kid was pictured standing next to his father on a seashore, the night sky above them exploding with light. Was it a shell? Or was it something the universe had sent, like in the other comic books he'd read this month? Robert took a deep breath and opened the comic.

The Maple Leaf Kid was with his father on an unnamed island in the Mediterranean. They were helping the Allies locate the plans for a new and lethal weapon of terrible destructive power. But they were too late. The weapon had been built and was ready to be used against our Canadian boys! They would have to destroy it. The Kid figured the exact trajectory to send the weapon hurtling into space instead – directly into the heart of an oncoming meteor shower. As he knew would happen, it was struck by a meteor, blowing it to bits. A brilliant fireball lit up the night sky, allowing the Canadian troops to spot and capture the Nazi scientists as they made their escape.

Robert closed the comic book. Very satisfying. He felt his own lucky star tingling as it hung from its silver chain around his neck. There was no mistaking the story line. It had involved the Mediterranean, and where were Sicily and Italy?

The part that truly counted was how a meteor had saved the day. How could all three comics have a meteor in them at the same time?

He found his latest copies of *Captain Ice* and *Sedna of the Sea*, placing them in a row next to *The Maple Leaf Kid*, admiring the artwork.

Retrieving his brothers' letters from the dresser, Robert took George's out and reread it. The part about doing the steep climb, then the roll and dive fit perfectly with Ice's adventure.

He placed George's letter beside the air ace's bright cover.

Next was James and his bees that had turned out to be mines, exactly like Sedna and her submarine trap. He put James' letter with Sedna.

This was like the plot from a science-fiction novel. He tried to be logical, only logic was long gone.

Patrick's letter rested on top of *The Maple Leaf Kid* with its fireball cover glowing at him from the faded bedspread.

It wasn't a coincidence.

There was something going on here, something he was supposed to pay attention to and it was huge.

Patrick had seen a meteorite the same night Robert had seen his. He took his chain off and held the fallen star. It felt warm as it nestled contentedly in his palm. It had been this meteorite. It had to be, and it was a cosmic connection between him and his brothers. The universe meant for him to find this speck of stardust, and the comic books were pointing at the connection, plain as the iron rock he now held.

His heroes were showing him what was happening to his brothers and how they would get out of whatever trouble hit them! He felt dizzy. Maybe he was crazy. Robert's gaze went from the comic book covers to his brothers' letters. Maybe he wasn't.

Who was he to say how the mysteries of the universe worked? All he knew was he'd been given a special insight, a gift, and he shouldn't dismiss it. His superheroes were here to help.

Robert came to a decision, one that could get him a one-way ticket to the loony bin if anyone found out. He also knew it was the most important decision of his life.

Somehow, the fantasy comic book world and the real world of his brothers had fused. Robert's part in this cosmic connection was to ensure he always had the latest editions of his heroes' adventures. He was positive of this. Secretly, he'd always thought he belonged in a different universe, and now he had the chance to do something as big and as unknown as the vast Milky Way galaxy itself.

"Captain Ice," he brusquely addressed the image of the air hero. "I'm assigning you to guard my brother George. I want you to accompany him on his missions and report back to me next month with any news." Robert took the comic and the letter to the dresser and put them next to George's picture.

"Sedna of the Sea, please watch over James. He doesn't always make the best decisions and could use your wisdom." He took Sedna and the letter from James to the dresser and arranged them next to his brother's picture.

Returning to his bed, Robert sat beside the remaining comic book. "Kid, you know you're my favourite hero." He touched the brightly coloured cover. "Don't tell my other brothers, but Patrick is the pick of the litter as far as I'm concerned and I'd really appreciate it if you could keep him safe, as a personal favor to me." He walked to the dresser, moved Patrick's smiling picture between his other two brothers and their comic book guardians, and then carefully placed the latest edition of *The Maple Leaf Kid* and Patrick's letter against the picture frame.

He stepped back from the dresser and crisply saluted his cadre of heroes, all six of them. They were a team, a super team, brought together by forces none of them could fathom. One thing was certain – he would listen to that message from the void. He was the link between the two worlds and he would do his best to help with their fight.

As Robert went downstairs, he could feel his star buzzing around his neck.

CHAPTER EIGHT

BATTLE BEGINS

AS ROBERT SAT with his parents and ate dinner, he tried not to betray his new galactic status. He was acutely aware he was *different*, not daring to use the word *special*, and hoped his mother, who could spot a molecule out of place, didn't notice anything.

Now that he'd had his interstellar revelation, it was critical that he did not miss one single episode of his heroes' adventures. His mission was simple. He would win the grease contest. It would give him the money he'd need to keep the flow of comics coming, allowing his superheroes to continue their watch over his brothers.

Charlene Donnelly was an obstacle. He, however, would use his skill and cunning to show Crazy Charlie how it was done.

"Robert, stop gulping your food, for heaven's sake. You'll make yourself sick." His mother poured him a glass of milk.

"I have to eat fast Mum. I'm in this contest to collect fat for the war effort and I'm going to canvass the neighbourhood for grease and lard. There must be loads out there and after supper, when busy mothers are cleaning up the cooking mess, I'm sure they'll be more than happy for me to take the stuff away."

"That's a very good thing to do." His father, William, spoke up in his gravelly baritone. Tall and angular like his sons, his hair had gone grey early, which made him appear older than he was. "Our boys need more bombs and that means we all have to do our part. Tell you what son, I'll help with the dishes tonight so you can get on with your collecting."

Robert wondered if he'd heard right. This was an unexpected bonus he wasn't about to turn down. He'd take advantage of his father's generous, and highly unusual, offer. He'd also check the sky for a blue moon while he was doing his grease collecting.

For the rest of the evening Robert knocked on every door along his street and explained what he needed and why. Everyone was very generous. Old Mrs. Tate gave him a tub of grease she'd been saving for a donkey's age and when he went to the boarding house at the corner, Mrs. Johnson forked over a pail that must have weighed three pounds. She said it was lucky he'd come by as she'd been planning to take the gelatinous goo to the collection depot the following day.

He fell asleep that night in the middle of calculating how much fat would go to school with him tomorrow.

THE NEXT MORNING Robert found riding on a bicycle while balancing a load of slimy sludge to be quite a challenge. A couple of times, he had to get off and push so he wouldn't spill any of the precious cargo. When he hauled his cans into the school, he saw he'd collected way more than the other kids he met in the halls.

Smiling broadly, Robert felt the tiniest bit smug as he pushed open the doors to the home ec room.

The smile died on his lips and took the smug with it.

At the front desk, Charlie Donnelly stood next to a beat-up red wagon piled high with tubs and buckets. There was enough fat to build an entire arsenal, with a pound or two left over for a few extra firecrackers!

"Yow, Charlie – I mean *Charlene* – that's a ton of fat!" Robert's shock turned to irritation when he saw several of the pails had Hamburger Heaven written on the sides. That must be the name of the restaurant where her uncle worked, and with the amount he'd given her, the term "greasy spoon" slid to a whole other level. Charlie turned to him. "Gee, it might take a while to weigh all this. I seem to have an awful lot. You can leave your little tins and Miss Pettigrew will get to them later." Her smirk was all sticky sweet sugar.

"Oh I wouldn't dream of leaving." He smiled back, turning on his own maple syrup tap. "A couple of these babies are pretty heavy and I wouldn't want Miss Pettigrew to strain herself lifting."

Charlie's eyes glinted like shards of blue ice. "We had the same problem. Simple fix. We moved the scale to the floor, then worked together to drag the heaviest buckets onto the tray for weighing." Here, she wiped imaginary sweat from her brow. "Phew! There were a couple of doozies."

Miss Pettigrew raised her head from her calculations. "Charlene, you have fourteen pounds here! I must say, this is a marvellous start. Well done my dear." She pulled a pencil out of the haystack on her head and marked the number first on a clipboard which she kept hidden, then added the amounts to a giant thermometer chart on the wall. Other students' contributions were shaded in already.

The thermometer recordings were in different colours, and Robert decided it depended on which pencil his teacher laid her hands' on and not which student was being recorded since no names were shown on the big chart. Charlie's total was in bright red, like a big red stoplight – stopping him from winning, stopping him from collecting his comic books and stopping him from helping his brothers!

Grinning like a Cheshire cat, Crazy Charlie waltzed out of the room humming, "We're in the Money."

Robert set his buckets down. "Would you like me to move the scale to the floor?" he asked, seeing it was back on the counter.

Miss Pettigrew eyed Robert's offering. "Nope, won't be necessary."

His total was seven pounds, which was way less than he'd thought. Crazy Charlie was already so far in front of him, he couldn't even see her tail lights. He'd have to come up with a better battle plan.

Later that night, as he explained his problem of needing more fat to his comic book commandos, he held his meteorite tightly in his fist and wished for help, squeezing it so hard it left indentations in his palm.

ROBERT RECEIVED HIS HELP when he discovered no other kids in his neighbourhood were entering the contest, so he could canvass their streets as well. He expanded his search area, collecting every ounce of lard, fat, sludge and goo, but still he was behind his arch enemy. On Friday morning, he was at this locker when Crazy Charlie stopped by.

"I know what I'm getting...*ka-ching!* I wonder if they'll have a Thanks for Your Feeble Effort ribbon for the rest of you losers. Unless of course, you've got a real *fat bomb* at home you're waiting to bring in?"

Robert slammed his locker door shut. She was fishing for information. Silly girl. He wasn't about to give anything away. "Hey, how's tricks Char-lean?" He hoped she'd get his subtle reference to her stick-skinny build.

"Cut the rapier wit, Tourond. I saw your total and I'd say things are lookin' mighty good – *for me.*"

He wondered how she knew his total, since the all-important clipboard was kept locked in Miss Pettigrew's desk. He decided his devious and, he had to admit, clever foe must be watching when kids brought their donations in and figuring out their amounts from the coloured bands marked on the wall chart. Actually, this wasn't a bad idea. Robert decided he would add it to his strategy as well.

"Don't be so sure..." And here he rubbed his shoulder like it was sore. "I've got a load at home to bring in and my arm still aches from lifting it."

She snorted. "With those pipe cleaner arms, I'm sure it must be all of two pounds." She tossed her long ponytail over her shoulder and, before Robert could think of a cutting response, waltzed away down the hall. He knew he had an edge: his interstellar pendant. Every time he held the meteorite and really concentrated, something good happened. For instance, several times while out canvassing the neighbourhood yesterday, he'd touched his talisman and *poof!* the lady of the house would remember a pail in the basement or a can of bacon grease she'd set aside.

At the end of the day, as Robert was slipping the stone back on before he went home, a couple of his classmates came over and said he could have whatever they collected that weekend as they wanted him to beat Crazy Charlie. Robert had a moment of discomfort; he didn't think the contest was supposed to be about popularity. Then he remembered that lives were at stake and he accepted their offers.

He canvassed all weekend, yet even with the donations of his friends, the battle almost turned into hand-to-hand combat on Monday morning when Charlie hauled in a wagon stacked so high with the precious goop, she'd had to tie it down with ropes.

"Man, I didn't think I'd make it in. I'm going to have to get a bigger wagon!" Charlie's hair was plastered to her forehead with sweat, like she'd run a race against Jesse Owens.

Robert again noticed the Hamburger Heaven logo. He wished he had a few convenient family connections in the dining industry, but refrained from commenting and dug in for a hard fight.

He'd added a respectable number of pounds to his total, but when Charlie brought another load in Tuesday, he could see he needed to score big. If his nemesis continued to use her uncle's restaurant, then Robert would have to do something spectacular or he wasn't going to win, which meant no Maple Leaf Kid, not to mention Sedna or Ice. He thought of his brothers' being left unprotected and shuddered. He couldn't let that happen.

TUESDAY EVENING THE PHONE rang and Robert ran to get it. "Hello? Tourond residence, Robert speaking." When his parents bought their telephone, his mother had insisted he answer in this stuffy way. Personally, he thought he sounded like a butler from Buckingham Palace.

"Hi Robbie, it's Katy."

Kathryn Tourond Thibault was Robert's first cousin once removed, and although she was older even than his father and they didn't see each other nearly often enough, Katy was his all-time favourite relative. She was also the only person on the planet who called him Robbie. Kathryn was a lawyer, a rare thing for a woman. She lived in River Falls, several hours drive from Calgary. The long-established shantytown perched precariously in cleared areas on each side of the road and had few amenities for these people who lived on the edge of society. In recent years, though, conditions had improved a lot, and his cousin was in a large part responsible. She fought for something called "civil rights" and Robert envied her bravery. Katy was the very definition of a true superhero.

"Hey cuz. What's up?" he asked cheerily.

"I'll be in Calgary on Thursday with work and thought I'd come for dinner and stay the night, if it's agreeable with your mother."

"Mum will be over the moon! She's done with her experimental cooking using Spork: 'the meat of many uses.' She has a new recipe called Shipwreck – seven layers of all the macaroni, hamburger, corn, peas and other assorted flotsam and jetsam you can handle," Robert joked. He continued listing their probable menu. "This will be followed by her famous eggless spice cake. It really sticks to your ribs and will take up homesteading in your stomach. And you'll also have all the tea you can drink. Rationing is in full swing here in Calgary and Mum says we're down to bare bones."

"Well, that sounds better than fricasseed gopher, the tough-times dish you get around here." Kathryn's joke had a dark edge, referring as it did to her beloved road-allowance people; then she brightened. "Your mother's recipes sounds delicious, Robbie! I can hardly wait to be shipwrecked. And the cake? Well now, I call any cake my friend. How about you – what's new?"

Robert touched his pendant. "I'm glad you asked. I found an actual meteorite. Mr. G, our neighbour, thinks it's mostly iron and it is heavy. It's the neatest thing I've ever had. He made it into a sort of necklace and I wear it all the time." He was excited to talk to someone about it and could hardly wait until Thursday so he could show it to her. He'd leave out the comic book connection, though. Even she wouldn't believe him and they'd been friends since Moby Dick was a guppy!

"A real meteorite! That is fascinating. I look forward to all the exciting details. Have you heard anything from your brothers?"

"Yup. They're all doing fine and having so many adventures that Mum is in a constant panic. You know how she gets when she thinks any of her boys are having too much fun. It's..."

"*Practically sinful!*" Katy and Robert both said this at the same time, then burst into laughter.

"And, speaking of your brothers, I have something special for Patrice. Your grandmother Belle and I have been doing some fall cleaning at her place and found something we think he would love to have."

"Katy," Robert interrupted, "You know he goes by Patrick."

This was a long-standing family battle. Patrick said *Patrice* sounded foreign: the name Patrick was more English and easier for people to say. But Robert thought his brother was worried that people would ask him about his family's ancestry. The Tourond's were Métis, a mix of Native and French Canadian. Robert was proud they could trace their roots to the days of the fur trade and the Hudson's Bay and North West Companies, but Patrick was not. Families were complicated and so were family histories.

"I know all about hiding our roots, Robbie." The darkness in her voice was back. "My father did exactly the same thing with his name and for the same reasons. Passing for all white makes things go smoother. It's a shame Patrice –" she stopped herself – "*Patrick* feels he has to hide his heritage, which is why I'm bringing him a gift."

"A gift? What is it?" Robert was curious now. "Come on, you can tell me"

"You'll see," she trilled, the regretful tone gone.

Once his cousin made a decision, it was "discussion over" time. He'd have to wait and changed the subject. "How's Grandma? Still working harder than any three lumberjacks?"

"Of course!" Kathryn confirmed. "She sends her love and asks if you've been out hunting yet. She feels no self-respecting Métis boy should pass fifteen without bringing down his first *jumper*. That's a deer to you city slickers."

Robert harrumphed in a manly fashion. "Well, then I've still got a few months to bag my trophy winner."

At the mention of hunting, a wild idea started to swirl in his brain. Wild, yes, and one he'd gladly turn into a giant *kaboom!* for Charlie Donnelly. He gripped the receiver a little tighter. "Cuz, speaking of deer and bear and other greasy beasts, I have a huge favour to ask. I'm in a contest at school to see who can collect the most fat for the war effort. I would really appreciate it if you could ask your neighbours if they have any left over from all their wild meat."

There was a pause on the crackly line. "I don't know, Robbie, lots of folks here don't have the luxury of electric lights. They use the tallow to make candles. I'll ask, but I can't promise anything. Now, I'd best talk to your mum about staying."

Robert called his mother to the telephone. He felt very satisfied with himself despite Katy's caution. With luck, she would come through and Crazy Charlie would discover what the term "blown out of the water" meant. As a reward for his brilliant thinking, he decided to reread the Maple Leaf Kid's latest adventure for the hundredth time. As he entered his room, he touched his meteorite and felt it buzz in response.

CHAPTER NINE

A COUSIN COMES CALLING

THURSDAY MORNING, ROBERT'S total fat amounted to thirty-eight pounds while Charlie's was more than fifty. It wasn't looking good for him and his enemy sniffed victory like a bloodhound after a fox.

"I think I'll go to the pictures tonight," she said coolly as they both scrutinized the thermometer chart on the home ec wall. "I positively adore the movies and I certainly don't have to collect any more grease. There's probably no room for it in the storage closet anyway."

"Yup, probably not an inch of space. You may as well go." Robert agreed. He hated to admit he was getting a little nervous. Soon, the new editions of his superheroes' exploits would be in; he needed to have his deal with Mr. Kreller in place so he could bring his friends home, safe and sound.

"What's this? *The Superhero's Guide to Losing?*" Charlie snatched the copy of *The Maple Leaf Kid* sticking out of his back pocket. "I don't see what the big deal is with these things. There's no more than ten words on a page. Not exactly *War and Peace.*"

For Robert, this pushed the wrong button and pushed it hard. "You don't get it because your puny brain can't make the leaps it takes to follow the story without a million words. Anyway, the Maple Leaf Kid is a true Canadian hero. He's super smart and can solve any problem. He makes tools and complicated devices from ordinary stuff you'd find anywhere, like a crystal radio set out of pop bottle glass and wire. Best of all, the Kid is a teenager." He realized he was sounding a little insane and stopped talking.

"Ho hum," Charlie yawned as she paged through the comic. "So what's this stuff at the end of the book?"

Robert thought about clawing back his property and walking away, but decided to continue his rival's much needed education. "The Kid goes beyond the pages of the comic; he communicates with the readers themselves. See this...? He pointed out the final page. "It's the Maple Leaf Kid Fan Club. The Kid asks a question about something that happened in one of the earlier episodes and fans write in with their answer. If your letter is drawn and the answer is correct, you get a prize in the mail."

"So, have you ever sent in a right answer?" Charlie asked as she read the rules.

Robert hesitated and then figured there was no harm in admitting the truth. She was the first girl he'd ever known to show any interest in his comics, even if she was mocking them. "I'd rather keep the price of the stamp and put the money toward buying new comics instead."

He didn't bother telling her that a fan who did something super to help the war effort was spotlighted with a short feature article in the national comic book.

Robert slid a sideways peek at Charlie and thought of the Great Grease Roundup. When he won, this time he would write the fan club and tell them how he'd supported the war effort by collecting enough fat to build dozens of bombs. He'd be spotlighted for sure. That would be something! His brothers would be thrilled to see how hard he was fighting for them on the home front.

Charlie caught him looking at her. "I bet you're so lame, you imagine yourself in one of these." She tossed him back the comic. "You could be the Maple Leaf Kid's sidekick, the Poplar Punk or, more likely, the Unstoppable Wonder Weed. Yeah, that's you; *Wonder Weed*."

Robert cringed at the insulting nicknames.

Laughing maniacally, the evil scourge of the universe sauntered off.

IT WAS NEARING DINNER on Thursday when there was a knock at the front door.

"Robert, get that, dear. I'm busy with the cake," his mother called up to him.

Reluctantly, he put Ice back next to George's picture and went to see who was interrupting their adventure. When he opened the door, Kathryn waited on the porch.

Robert reached for her suitcase, then blurted out the one question he had to know the answer to. "So, were the generous people of River Falls able to help with my contest?"

She laughed. "My, you are eager. Don't worry; it's in the car." She hugged him. "How's my favourite little cousin?"

"Fine as frog's hair and not so little."

They immediately shared all the juicy news: how much school stank (it stank bad), who got married and had a baby (not necessarily in that order), his mother's Knit for Victory war effort (she was single-handedly defeating *that Hitler* with her dry socks), the biggest buck taken this season (twelve-point) and the hit of the whole conversation – his luckier-than-lucky find, the meteorite.

Admiring the pendant, Kathryn was genuinely impressed. "Goodness, it's a mini work of art, Robbie! How remarkable to have found it." She inspected more closely. "My, it seems to have a sort of glow, doesn't it?"

Robert had thought this too, but hadn't said anything in case he sounded like a lunatic. "Yeah, and it always feels warm. Weird, huh?"

Kathryn agreed. "Yes, definitely weird!"

"I'll take your suitcase to the spare room." He hoisted the bag and started up the stairs.

"If you're going to be a gallant gentleman and haul my bag, the least I can do is trail behind and act all swoony and ever so grateful." She laughed and pretended to fan herself, Southern belle-style.

Kathryn followed him to the back bedroom where Robert set the little suitcase onto a waiting chair. "Mum's put out towels for you on the bed and water in that carafe." He pointed out the linens and drinking water. "I'll let you unpack. See you downstairs."

"Actually, Robbie, can I talk to you for a minute?"

Robert heard something in her voice and stopped. "Sure, what's up?"

"This is between you and me, cousin to cousin. Agreed?"

Her tone was so serious he wondered if something was wrong back at River Falls. Maybe she needed his help. "You bet." He tried to sound caring. "You know I'd walk on hot coals for you, cuz. Well, at least warm water."

She smiled. "Thanks for that, Robbie." Kathryn took his hand and led him to the small alcove with the window seat. "When I spoke to your mother on Tuesday, she mentioned you might be having a tough go of it with your brothers all being away fighting. She said you spend a lot of time alone in your room with your comics."

This surprised Robert. He didn't think his mother noticed anything. "Yeah, so?" For some reason he felt defensive about his mother's monitoring what he did.

"Sweetheart, I understand how frightening the war must be for you. All three of your brothers are in constant danger. That's a lot of stress for anyone to handle and sometimes we need a friend to lean on."

Robert felt a lump spring into his throat.

"I want you to know that I'm here for you. We're family, and I think you and I are best friends, too. We stick together." She tipped her head. "Do you know why your mother had that telephone put in? She knew sooner or later, her little herd of boys would leave home and she wanted you to be able to call her whenever you needed to. I'm offering you the same deal – I'm here for you, day or night. If you're having a problem, I'm only a phone call away."

He nodded, understanding this offer came from love. "I might take you up on that sometime, if things with mum get too much!"

She patted his hands, then stood. "Good. And speaking of your mum...not a word to her about my spilling the beans. Okay?"

"Okay," he agreed as he followed her down stairs. Kathryn knew him well and she was very clever, yet he couldn't help wondering if he'd been set up for this little heart-to-heart.

DINNER WAS A COMPLETE SUCCESS with everyone raving over his mother's Shipwreck and asking for seconds. The cake was delicious too, despite its lack of eggs and the watery frosting.

Over their second pot of tea, Kathryn explained why she had come. "Aunt Belle and I are sure *Patrick*," she emphasized the name for Robert's benefit, "would like this." She reached into her carpet bag and withdrew a worn Red River sash. "It belonged to his namesake, my father Patrice, who also went by Patrick. This will help him remember where he comes from, and will also remind him we love him and are thinking of him. It's only an old sash and its real value is in the connection it has to family. This's why we think Patrick, fighting so far from home, needs something tangible to remind him he is not alone on the battlefield."

Taking the sash, Robert's father touched the faded arrow-head pattern with his calloused fingers. "I remember hearing stories of the old days when I was growing up. It was a hard life on the road allowances and many didn't survive for long. They were brave, smart and a lot tougher than most today."

Robert saw memories of those long ago tales cloud his father's face and it made him want to know more. He wished his dad would tell him those stories. He'd heard small pieces of how the road allowance settlers were on their own and at the mercy of unscrupulous thieves, farmers and merchants with no help from the law. The hunger and sickness, family triumphs and brutal losses: these tales were Metis history but were not written down anywhere. It made it all the more important to hear them so they wouldn't be forgotten entirely.

"Robbie," Kathryn interrupted his thoughts, "you and your brother have always been particularly close." She went on persuasively, "You could send the sash along with your next letter. He'd appreciate it coming from you."

Robert knew *no* was not an option with his cousin. "Sure, Katy, I'd be happy to."

He didn't think his brother would be thrilled to receive this particular gift, even with the attached loving sentiment.

CHAPTER TEN

AND THE WINNER IS

THE VISIT WENT LONG into the night and it was hard to get up for school the next morning. When Robert did finally drag himself out of bed, the first item on his agenda was to ask Kathryn about the grease. Today was Fat Day – the totals would be tallied and the winner announced.

Robert felt the weight of the chain around his neck and was sure Kathryn had come through.

When he came into the kitchen, his cousin was already finishing her breakfast. "Morning, cuz. So, the grease? How'd we do?"

"Oh, yes, Robbie. The messy stuff is in my car. Eat first, and then I'll show you." Kathryn sipped her tea. She was immaculately dressed in a perfectly tailored teal suit and looking very much the way he imagined a lady lawyer should.

Robert wolfed down his porridge and hurried to get his book bag. This was it. If his cousin had been successful with her collection, he was a winner in waiting.

Walking outside, Robert was aware of his special talisman tucked safely under his shirt. The big question was had she brought enough to win?

Kathryn went around the car, opening first the trunk, then the back doors. "You were lucky. Everyone had oodles of the stuff."

"Wham! Kablam!" Robert goggled. The car was jammed with big metal milk cans, at least seven of them! "Wow, thank you people of River Falls!"

"Jars wouldn't do it, so my clever husband used these. It started with two, then word spread and *voila!* I hope this helps." Kathryn scrutinized the cargo. "I think I should give you and all this grease a ride to school, or you won't get them weighed in time. You did say the contest closes this morning?"

"Yes, cut-off is the first bell. And yes again to the offer of hauling this freight for me, but I'll ride my bike, so I'll have it for the way home. Thanks, cuz. You're a peach."

He was feeling elated as he biked to school, leading his cousin behind him in her car like a drum major in a parade. He was sure the huge amount he was bringing would secure his win.

"Thanks again, Katy," Robert said for the millionth time as he lifted the heavy cans out of the trunk.

"Anything for my favourite little cousin." She tried to ruffle his extra-short hair. "Now, go empty the cans so I can bring them home with me."

Robert struggled into the school, a milk can dangling from each arm. They were truly heavy. Miss Pettigrew's carmine-coated mouth formed a perfect O when she saw him.

"My, my, *my!* Someone's been busy." She put the big scale on the floor and went to the storage room. Seconds later, she rolled out an enormous tub that must have come from an old washing machine and placed it on the scales. "I'll weigh the tub, then put your fat in and do the subtraction to calculate the total pounds of grease goodies. What a haul!" She was like a kid at Christmas as she transferred the contents of the milk cans.

"Hang on to your bonnet, Miss Pettigrew, 'cause this ride ain't over!" His teacher's giddiness was contagious and Robert hurried out with the empty cans, eager to bring in more.

He busily ferried in another set and his teacher squealed with delight. "We're going to kick the hiney of every school in the district. Wait till the next teachers' development day. Those harpies from Western Canada High School will have to find someone else to lord it over. We'll see who gets stuck with the title of School Least Likely this year."

As Robert was bringing in more cans, he passed Charlie Donnelly at the school doors, her book bag tied on her back so she could run more easily. He couldn't resist taunting her. "Hey, check out the *fat bomb* I found hanging around the house. This should help with the war effort." He felt like an air ace, returning home from an overwhelming victory – if he could have, he would have waggled his wings at her.

Charlie gaped, then a scowl darkened her face. "Those have fat in them?"

"You bet your skinny...ah, yah, they sure do." Robert continued down the hallway with his load of grease, trying not to sweat too hard in front of his competition. "You know, a little here, a little there, every ounce helps." This time he couldn't help it, he gave her a full-on victory roll, spinning around with the cans outstretched from his sides.

Too late, he felt his arms pulling in opposite directions, the heavy cans acting like shot-put hammers as he spun faster and faster, out of control. With a mortifying bang, Robert smashed open the home ec doors, still whirling toward his teacher, who gave a terrified squeak, then fell back in shock.

The last thing Robert saw was Crazy Charlie Donnelly storming away.

He had no time to enjoy his enemy's retreat. His arms were being pulled out of their sockets and he had to save the grease. Dropping to his knees, Robert managed to slow his forward momentum and, with his last ounce of strength, he drew the cans toward him, sliding into an ancient cooking stove like a base runner into home plate. Safe!

Once order was restored, Miss Pettigrew gathered all of Robert's fat, including previous contributions, and dumped everything into the tub. And then she launched into a running commentary: *"And the long shot, Rocket Robert, surges from behind! The track favourite, Charming Charlene, can hear hoof beats closing. We're down to the final furlongs now, folks, and it's*

Charming Charlene, Charming Charlene. Wait a second! Here comes our dark horse Rocket Robert. And as they cross the finish line, it's..." She eyed the brimming vat. *"Stay tuned for the thrilling conclusion of our race."*

Robert was astounded. Could it be? Did Miss Pettigrew bet the ponies?

"I want the winner to be a surprise, even to me. I will do the final weigh-in of my two highest competitors at the assembly." His teacher scraped the last of Robert's jars with a pencil, deftly flicking the grease into the tub. "Then we'll see which horse ends up in the winner's circle."

Robert caught a quick look at the number on the scale and surreptitiously checked the chart on the wall for Charlie's last drop off. You could always tell which was hers as there would be a big solid-coloured section on the carefully calculated paper thermometer.

Since he'd seen Charlie coming into the school without her infamous red wagon, and now that he had his total, he already knew who the winner was. He started figuring out how many comic books he could buy once he cashed in all those stamps. With this single win, he would keep his heroes happy and his brothers safe for months.

As Robert strolled down the hallway, he stood a little taller, felt a little more confident and, when he passed a gaggle of cheerleader types, he touched the brim of an imaginary fedora. "Morning, ladies." This left them busily whispering and pointing after him.

As the clang of the class bell ricocheted off the corridor walls, Robert decided life was indeed sweet. His superhero buddies were going to pat him on the back when they found out what a "super" job he'd done in securing the funds to keep their lifeline strong.

THE GYMNASIUM BUZZED with excitement. The winner of the Great Grease Roundup was about to be announced. Robert walked in exuding confidence, which was not what he usually exuded in the gymnasium. On the stage, Miss Pettigrew fussed with a wide sheet of canvas covering something lumpy.

As he scanned the room, Robert spied Crazy Charlie, sitting by herself at the edge of the crowd. He went to join her.

"Come to see me win?" It was hard not to gloat a tiny bit as he sank down in the chair next to hers.

"I think that's my line." She shot back.

"Numbers don't lie, Charlie." He'd done the math; the win was his.

Miss Pettigrew moved to the front of the stage and the crowd stilled. His teacher's idea of sprucing up for the big reveal meant she'd stuck a dozen of her coloured pencils into her hair at all angles, nailing the haystack to the top of her head and making her appear like a Barnum and Bailey human pincushion.

Robert took his pendant out and held it. Now he understood how the comic books worked, today's victory was incredibly important.

"I want to thank all the students who participated," she began.

"You've made our school proud. In fact, I believe this is the most successful drive in the whole district! There were two competitors who managed to put us way over the target. Fabulous work, really..."

Robert was tempted to give the crowd a royal wave.

She brandished a piece of paper. "Here, I have the totals for the students in the contest." She proceeded to read out the names and amounts contributed by every student who had taken part, starting with a kid who brought in less than a cup full. Finally Miss Pettigrew reached the end of her list and neither Charlie nor Robert's totals had been read out.

"I must admit, I have kept the best for the last. Right up until this morning, I thought we had a clear winner. Nothing so easy. It turned into a very exciting sprint to the finish, boys and girls."

She must be talking about the Great Milk Can Delivery he'd pulled off. Robert felt the corners of his mouth inching upward. He did nothing to dissuade them.

"To add a little drama, I will do a public weighing of the top two contestants here in front of you all! This number will be final!" She walked over to the sheet shrouded display and tugged the cover off. There stood a tall upright weigh scale and, on either side, an enormous wash tub of fat. "May I have my assistants, please?"

Two burly students from the wrestling team climbed the steps and stood flanking the scale. "We shall now weigh the final two entries." She nodded to a kid sitting at the side of the stage and a loud drum roll filled the auditorium.

The muscle-bound assistants lifted one of the tubs and set it on the scale. Miss Pettigrew adjusted the slide, patiently watching the teetering balance, waiting for it to still, then marked a number on her clipboard.

"The official total for Robert Tourond is a staggering..."

Everyone held their collective breath.

"...sixty-three pounds!"

That wasn't quite what Robert had come up with this morning, but he was still sure he had the win. Like he'd said, numbers don't lie, and he had Charlie's number. The audience applauded this mammoth amount and he dropped his hold on the meteorite to give the V for Victory sign to his cheering fans.

The two students removed Robert's vat of fat and replaced it with Charlie's offering. Miss Pettigrew withdrew a fresh pencil from her hair and proceeded to fiddle with the scale.

Charlie turned to him, all nasty and no nice. "You think you're pretty smart."

Robert was about to say something when she spotted his pendant. "What's this?" She reached out and grabbed the meteorite. Peering closely, she scrutinized it.

"And for Charlene, the total is..." Their teacher adjusted the balance on the scale, wiggled the vat a little and rechecked the number before writing it down. "Oh, my! This is remarkable...and a bit of a surprise. Charlene Donnelly has sixty-three...no, sixty-*four* pounds!"

Charlie dropped the meteorite as the crowd burst into excited chatter.

Robert sat in shocked silence. Sixty-four pounds? She'd beaten him by *one whole pound?* Impossible! He was sure of his numbers and he knew his was the last delivery. He'd seen Charlie in the hall, and there was no way she would have had enough time to run out for more fat before the morning bell rang.

Charlie's mouth slid into a rock-hard line as she sat rigidly in her chair.

"Can both these students come up here, please?" Their teacher motioned expectantly at them.

Robert was numb. He couldn't believe he'd lost. Slowly, he rose to his feet and as he did, his necklace flashed. It hit him then. Charlie had been holding the talisman when they'd announced the winner! Had that somehow changed things? Had she stolen his good luck? Anger rose like bile. That was it! She had snatched the win from him as surely as she had snatched the pendant. He tucked the charm back inside his shirt, anger making him fumble with the chain.

Feeling like a prisoner, Robert stood silently, head down as he waited on the stage. He focussed on inspecting his worn shoes, inherited from Patrick, and noticed the end of one shoelace. The end pieces of shoelaces, what were they called again? He knew once. He tried to ignore the disturbing burning sensation in his eyes and desperately hoped it didn't turn into something truly embarrassing. That would be the final humiliation and he was sure his soul-sucking classmates would love to add Blubber Boy and Snot-Nosed Loser to their repertoire of names for him.

Miss Pettigrew went on in her husky smoker's rasp. "As we want to acknowledge both of you for your valiant efforts, the staff has decided there will be *two prizes.*"

Robert's head snapped up. Were they going to give him a book of those lifesaving little stamps after all? Were his black-and-white heroes still going home with him? Would they continue to guard his brothers and keep them safe?

"For our runner-up, Robert Tourond, we have a war savings stamp book also..."

He leaned forward.

"With *two stamps* to get him started!"

There were a few boos, quickly stifled by a glare from the principal and the clapping of the crowd. A wave of disappointment choked Robert. He hiccupped, feeling heartsick. Two stamps would do him no good. Mr. Keller had been very specific about accepting only a full book!

He remembered his plan to send his victory story to the Maple Leaf Kid Fan Club. Like that would ever happen now.

The worst thing, the thing that made him sweat, was the loss meant the comic book connection that kept his brothers' safe was in deadly jeopardy.

His teacher motioned him forward to the microphone as she gave him his consolation prize.

The crowd waited for his acceptance speech. Robert surveyed the sea of faces and opened his mouth to say thank you. Unfortunately, it wasn't only his heart that was sick. An enormous belch erupted from his roiling stomach, and the noise echoed around the auditorium like a bomb going off. The entire room burst into raucous laughter, wolf whistles and foot stomping. His mortification complete, Robert shuffled back without uttering a word.

Charlie stepped forward to accept her prize – *his* prize. He'd thought she'd be dancing a jig or at least be more gracious about her win. Instead, she stared steadfastly at the war savings stamps as she received them and then mumbled a thank-you into the microphone that he was sure no one heard since they were still howling at his more than memorable speech.

On the long ride home, Robert's mind whirled as he tried to think up another way to find the money for his comic books. He felt like his brothers' lives depended on it. His feelings for Crazy Charlie Donnelly nosedived even farther.

CHAPTER ELEVEN

ROYAL MISS

AT SUPPER, ROBERT'S MOTHER was thrilled with the stamps.

"This is perfect timing!" she gushed, inspecting his prize. "I'm going to buy more with your allowance and, when you've filled the book, then we'll purchase your first war savings certificate! We won't stop there. We'll continue buying stamps, as many as we can. Isn't that wonderful?"

Robert didn't know what to say. His mother had no idea what the consequences of his losing could be.

THE RELENTLESS ENEMY HARRIED OUR HERO, AN UNENDING SUPPLY OF BULLETS SLAMMED INTO HIS LITTLE FIGHTER. THE ENEMY`S SOLE PURPOSE – TO SEND HIM DOWN IN FLAMES!

His father was no help either. "I think it makes sense. Your money will make money, so to speak." He reached for the Steak Surprise his mother had made for dinner. The surprise being it wasn't steak. Instead, it was some mystery meat that smelled suspiciously like fried Spork.

OUR HERO KNEW HE WAS OUTGUNNED – ANY CHANCE OF VICTORY GROUND TO DUST BY THE MERCILESS JAWS OF

DEFEAT. THE END WAS COMING AND HE COULD DO
NOTHING TO STOP IT!

His mother unexpectedly changed topics, coming in for another attack. "Robert, do you have your parcel ready to be mailed to Patrick?"

"It's on the sideboard in the hall," he answered, chewing on the rubbery mush as his tongue searched futilely for a morsel of real steak.

"Don't talk with your mouth full. I'll mail it with my letter which means I'd better hear back from him the same time you do, Robert, or I'll want to know why." She turned to his father. "William, you must speak to those boys of yours and explain how I wait for the postman every day, *every blessed day*, William, to bring me news from them. Even a postcard would do!"

Once Robert's mother started telling his dad to "speak to those boys of yours," he knew he was home free. He could melt into his own thoughts.

NO ONE WAS SAFE FROM THE ENEMY'S GUNS, EVEN A
DEFENCELESS CIVILIAN. OUR HERO USED A FRIENDLY
CLOUD BANK TO SLIP OUT OF HIS ENEMY'S GUNSIGHTS.

Robert had spent a couple of evenings writing his brother a long letter, encoding the good stuff, and then tried to find a way to explain the Métis sash included in the parcel. He was sure Patrick would give it back to Kathryn as soon as he came home. Robert had decided he'd ask his cousin if he could have the sash, as he liked the idea of being linked to history, especially his own family history.

WEEKENDS WERE USUALLY nothing special for Robert. On this particular Saturday, however, there was a glimmer of excitement in the air. A special train was to come through Calgary with members of the royal family aboard. Not King George, of course, only some relative. In social studies, they'd discussed the long succession of kings and queens who had ruled Canada and the British Empire and the way nobles in England came into the world with a title, land and privileges. Robert had been intrigued with the idea of being "blue-blooded" and wanted to see if these visitors looked any different from regular people. "Mum, I'm leaving. Be back later!" he called, grabbing his coat. He was almost at the kitchen door when his mother's disembodied voice thundered down from somewhere above, not unlike a command from the gods on Mount Olympus.

"Not before you finish your chores, young man. That's the rule for Saturdays and I see no reason to change it."

OUR HERO WAS TOTALLY UNPREPARED FOR THE SUDDEN ATTACK. THE ENEMY PLANE CAME OUT OF THE SUN AND OPENED UP WITH ITS HELLFIRE GUNS. AGAIN, OUR HERO'S PLANS WERE ABOUT TO BE BLASTED TO SMITHEREENS!

"Wham! Kablam!" Robert cursed. This was no time for household drudgery, and since his allowance now went to buying lousy stamps, it wasn't like he got to enjoy the fruits of his labours. "But, Mum, the royals! I'll do my chores later, I promise!"

He knew the train was scheduled for only a brief stop at noon so Mayor Davidson could meet the dignitaries before they continued their sightseeing trip through the scenic Rockies, always popular with fancy folk. It would take him fifteen minutes to bike to his secret hideout, which would be perfect for watching the festivities. Worryingly, the clock said it was 11:05 already. His comfortable margin was shrinking fast.

Sometimes, his mother could be relentless, and this was one of those times. "Chores first, Robert. No arguments."

"If I do them now, Mum, I'll miss the royal train! We talked about the monarchy in class. It's part of our studies." He hoped the mention of school would help his case.

His mother didn't take the bait.

WITH AN EVIL LAUGH, THE ENEMY SWOOPED IN, BRANDISHING A SECRET WEAPON TOO POWERFUL TO DEFEAT. OUR HERO WATCHED HELPLESSLY AS VICTORY WAS SNATCHED FROM HIS GRASP.

"We mustn't shirk our work. *William – tell your son!*"

His father had been fixing the screen door in the kitchen, blissfully unaware he was about to be drawn into the battle. It didn't take him long to join the fray.

"You heard your mother. Work then play, always in that order, son. A valuable life lesson you'll appreciate as you grow older." He went back to the screen, guarding Robert's escape route with the doggedness of St. Peter at the pearly gates.

Resigned to his fate, Robert tried to finish his list of jobs as fast as possible. Despite his father's words about the correct order to do things, he was so frustrated he could have exploded like a supernova. What did his mother know about work, anyway? She stayed home all day knitting and listening to her radio programs.

Finally, at twenty minutes to twelve, Robert was out the newly fixed door and speeding as fast as he could for his secret hideout, the deserted water tower behind the train station. He'd been going there for years and enjoyed the way it made him feel like a superhero, keeping watch high above the city, where nothing could touch him and he was free. There was barely time to make it.

He sped along the shadowed passageway provided by the tall fence that separated the rail yard from the adjacent roads. The dark tunnel was cool in the heat of the midday sun. Robert peddaled harder, leaning over the handlebars as the scream of the whistle announced the arrival of the special train. Ahead, he saw the rope ladder leading up to his lofty vantage point.

Beyond the wooden palisade, he heard the whoosh of the steam engine pulling into the station. It was impossible to see what was going on because of the high fence. Still, if he climbed fast enough, he'd have the perfect view. Skidding his bike to a stop, he leapt off and was reaching for a rung when the ladder was suddenly jerked up and out of his grasp.

Robert was momentarily confused. He was sure no one else knew about this place. "Hey, what's going on? Who's up there?" He waited impatiently. Nothing.

As he watched, a hand extended out from the walkway that ran around the base of the huge cistern high above. In it was a flask. As if in slow motion, the container was tipped. Liquid poured in a silvery cascade down, down, down...and over Robert, making him splutter. Fortunately, from the taste, the liquid was only water. It could have been a lot worse.

Then he heard it – a high, crazy laugh. A chill went down his spine. He'd know that cackle anywhere.

"Charlie Donnelly, you sad bag of bones! Lower the ladder right now!" There was no reply from above. Robert checked to his left, then his right. The long wooden fence extended far in each direction, and by the time he got his bike and rode to either end, the train would be gone.

"I'm giving you five seconds, *or else!*" Robert knew the "or else" was a hollow threat. It would have been more effective if he'd had a bazooka.

The ladder failed to appear.

From the other side of the fence, he heard the sound of metal wheels struggling on metal rails. It was the engine pulling out of the station. He'd missed his chance to see royalty and who knew when anyone important would come to Calgary again. "Wham! Kablam!" he cursed, picking up his bicycle again. He had to get out of there – if he stayed until Crazy Charlie came down from her ivory tower, he might forget he was raised to never slug a girl.

As ROBERT WAS PUTTING his bike in the garage, Mr. Glowinski walked out of his, wiping his hands on a rag.

"Robcio, on this beautiful day, why so sad?"

Robert puffed out his breath. "Ever had trouble with girls, Mr. G?"

The big man concentrated on removing one last speck of grime from his palm. "Tak, tak, once upon a time, long ago."

"Then you know how aggravating they can be and how sometimes you want to smack them so hard...."

"No, Robcio, never do that! A real man does not "smack them so hard." A real man finds way to make things better with his mind. *Tak?*"

"Oh, you mean outsmart the devils." Robert liked this approach.

"Not 'devils'. Girl can be mother, wife, sister, daughter and, for you, sweetheart."

Robert snorted. "That will be the day. I've had my fill of their kind."

Mr. G pursed his lips. "*Zabawny chlopak.* You pretty young to be monk, Robcio. Maybe give it year or two."

Robert ignored him. He was on a roll. "There's this really annoying girl, her name is Charlene, but everyone calls her Crazy Charlie and for a good reason. She beat me in this contest I really had to win, and today, she was in my secret place and wouldn't let me up. I missed the royals because of her."

"So, you lose in fair contest and then she beat you to 'secret place'. Maybe her 'secret place,' too."

This hadn't crossed his mind. Charlie had beaten him by one stinking pound, weighed in front of everyone. And she certainly was weird enough to know about the hideout at the top of the old tower. He kicked a pebble in the gravelled alley; his anger blowing away like thistledown in the wind. "Okay, I won't smack her, but I don't have to like her."

"No smacking, that is good thing. Maybe soon, when you older, you will change mind about girls."

"Don't bet on it, Mr. G." Robert waved goodbye and went into his house. As the door closed behind him, he thought he heard someone say, "Good bet, I think."

CHAPTER TWELVE

FASTER THAN A SPEEDING BIKE

ROBERT AWOKE MONDAY thinking how on earth was he going to pay for the October editions of his heroes when they came in? Worry continued to plague him as he biked to school. He knew his friendly neighbourhood pharmacist would never hold three comic books until he had the cash to buy them.

He'd been late leaving home this morning and hadn't bothered to tuck his pants into his socks. Big mistake. Without warning, he felt the tug of the bike chain as it gobbled up a loose trouser leg.

"Wham! Kablam!" Robert bumped over the curb and wobbled onto the sidewalk. Carefully, he back peddled until the chain coughed up the mangled material, now covered in grease and with a small nick out of the cuff. He'd been lucky. He could have taken a bad fall and his pants might have been ripped a lot worse. He'd heal, but torn pants meant dealing with Mother the Mender again, and he wanted to avoid that minefield at all costs. He'd have to try to disguise the nick before she spotted it and confiscated his bike as a radical safety strategy. Her poor little boy could fall and bruise his knee or kidnappers might steal his bike with him perched upon it!

Robert leaned his bike against a storefront and started picking off as much grime as possible. He tucked his pant legs in where they belonged and was about to resume his trek for school when a small sign at the bottom of the store window caught his eye. The glass was smudged, making it hard to see and harder to read. Wiping away the grime, Robert felt his heart leap.

WANTED: TELEGRAM DELIVERY BOY
AFTER SCHOOL WORK
APPLY MONDAY FOUR O'CLOCK P.M.
MUST HAVE OWN BICYCLE!

He read the sign above the door. It was the Canadian Pacific Telegraphs office!

It was as if the sun had burst out from behind a thundercloud. This was the answer to his prayers! He'd get a job as a telegram messenger. He had a great bicycle and knew the city like he'd built it. He'd have money and his mother would no longer be in control. She wanted him to grow up and take more responsibility, well, now he would do it in spades.

Robert reread the wording on the poster, *Wanted: Telegram Delivery Boy.* Boy singular, as in one position only. And he would be that telegram delivery boy, come hell or high water. This time, he wouldn't lose.

He'd be there at four. Heck, he'd be there at three if it would help. Feeling better than he had in days, he pushed off for school, his lucky talisman humming against his chest.

THE FINAL BELL RANG and Robert bolted out of the school like a race horse at a gate, then peddaled madly for home. Changing into his Sunday Mass white shirt and tie, he flew to the telegraph office, arriving in record time. As he wiggled his bike into the rack out front, he saw another, beat-up wreck already parked there. It was an old, balloon tire cruiser and must have been rescued from the city dump. If this was his competition's wheels, he was sure to win the position. Why would anyone want to use such a relic? It weighed about the same as a battleship.

Brushing back his short hair, Robert checked his reflection in the window to make sure his tie was straight, then marched boldly in...and stopped dead in his tracks.

Crazy Charlie Donnelly was sitting on a bench beside the door. Turning at the sound of his noisy entrance, his nemesis spied him and, immediately, her face took on a hard look. She was ready for battle.

"What are you doing here? Got tired of gloating about your fat win or sitting in your castle turret?" He knew he wasn't being polite, but so what? She was Satan's favourite and they both knew it.

"It's a telegraph office. Maybe I'm going to send a telegram." Her voice was steely.

"Sure you are. Well, don't let me stop you. Go ahead." He had a nasty suspicion why she was here, and it had nothing to do with *sending* telegrams and everything to do with *delivering* them. He pointed at the sign on the wall. "It says 'To send a telegram, ring the bell and someone will be with you shortly.' So ring the bell, Charlie."

She was busted. She'd cleaned herself up and put on different clothes, but not any girl clothes he'd seen before. She had on dungarees and a blue shirt. The entire outfit had every appearance of belonging to an older brother. Her long hair was shoved up under a tweed cap, like a boy would wear.

At that moment, an elderly gentleman entered the room from an office at the back. He was rather portly and held a fat, unlit cigar between his teeth. "Are you here for the job?"

Both Robert and Charlie jumped forward. "Yes, sir!" they said in unison.

The old gent's caterpillar eyebrows crawled up his forehead. "Nice to see such enthusiasm. The thing is, there's only one position open, fellas."

"I was here first, sir," Charlie volunteered. "My name is Charlie Donnelly and I am ready and able to work."

Charlie? Robert knew she hated the name. Then he realized – with the cap and the dungarees, she was hoping to pass for a boy.

"And my name is Robert Tourond and I can out-work Char*lene* any day of the week. She shouldn't even be here. The sign said delivery *boy* and she's a girl, Mr....ah..." Robert fumbled for the missing name.

"It's Crabtree, Mr. Crabtree, to you and I'm the telegraphist here." He chewed on his cigar as he appraised Charlie, who didn't appear particularly girlish in the rough trousers and shirt. "Now I have a better gander, you certainly are a girl." He chuckled, a deep rumbling noise like a John Deere tractor starting up. "Never thought about hiring a female before."

"I know the city, Mr. Crabtree." Charlie spoke quickly in her defence. "And I'm as fast as any boy."

"Not on the old wreck I saw outside," Robert interjected, cutting her off before she could say anything more. "It's a junker."

"Oh, yeah? Well, I can beat you any day of the week!" she boasted, but they both knew it wasn't going to happen that day.

"Whoa, now hold on, the pair of you." Mr. Crabtree's words ended the fight and sent them both to their corners. "I'm not sure a girl would be fast enough. We can't keep people waiting for their news while you put on fresh rouge."

Charlie tensed and her lips formed into the tight line Robert had seen before when she was really ticked off. He couldn't imagine her wearing rouge any more than he could picture a grizzly bear in a tutu.

"Now, now, no need to get huffy, young lady; I can see you don't use the stuff." The stout gent rolled the cigar from one side of his mouth to the other. "We'll decide this the good old-fashioned way." He walked over to the counter and wrote on two pieces of telegram paper, then folded the notes and sealed them.

"The first one to deliver his – or *her* – telegram, will get the job." He passed them each an envelope.

Both applicants stood looking at him, dutifully holding their letters.

"Well, what in Jehoshaphat's glorious green garden are you waiting for?" Mr. Crabtree exploded, the cigar wagged up and down like a scolding finger. "Shoo!"

Robert bolted for the door with Charlie in hot pursuit. They pushed and elbowed each other, trying to get the advantage. Robert didn't give an inch – this was no time to be a gentleman. This was war.

"Nice bike," he taunted as he grabbed his own shining ride. "Did Noah have a spare on the ark?"

He was off before Charlie had a chance to reply, his Raleigh light years faster than her clunker. Checking the address written on the telegram, he saw it was down by the new Colonel Belcher Hospital, about fifteen minutes away, maybe less if he caught the lights right.

He was confident this job was his. Maybe he could start today.

Since he was almost an official telegram delivery boy, Robert felt he was allowed to bend the rules of the road a little as he split the lanes on Fourth Street. Ahead, he saw the railway tracks and, worst luck, there was a long, *long* freight train dawdling past.

Impatiently, he waited as precious seconds ticked by. "Come on, come on, you rusty pile of scrap," he muttered under his breath.

Finally, the track cleared and Robert sped forward, legs churning. He narrowly missed a woman who stepped out from the sidewalk and walked directly into his path. "Hey, lady, the crosswalk's at the corner!" he yelled in his best delivery boy style as he dodged around her.

At last he saw the street he needed, then the house he wanted, and then, coming from a side street ahead of him...Charlie Donnelly, wheeling up to the same address!

He couldn't believe it. How had she done it? What kind of wings had she stolen to pull this miracle off?

Sliding to a stop, he reached for the gate latch as Charlie leapt the fence and sprinted ahead of him. He raced after her, vaulting up the steps of the veranda to stand beside her in front of the wooden door. They both knocked, and then waited for someone to answer their summons.

The door was opened by an elderly and very diminutive lady,

who peered up at them through glasses with round black rims, which reminded Robert of a little owl. Immediately, both Charlie and Robert stepped forward. "Telegram delivery, ma'am!" they chimed in unison as they thrust their letters out in front of them.

She tut, tutted. "My, this will make it tricky. Come in, children, come in." She swung the screen door wide and they entered the bright hallway. "Cyrus telephoned to say you were coming."

She used a cane as she hobbled over to the wall where a black telephone waited. "I'll let him know you've arrived." She whirled the crank on the phone and told the operator the number she needed.

Robert could hear the ringing at the other end.

"Hello, dear. Your telegrams have arrived."

Muffled words issued from the receiver.

"I couldn't say, Cyrus. When I opened the door, they were both standing there like two peas in a pod." She paused, listening; then nodded as if Mr. Crabtree could somehow see her. "Yes, I thought it a might unusual, too. You'd be the first." A thundered reply had Mrs. Crabtree holding the instrument away from her ear. "Yes, yes, I think that's the best choice, dear."

She hung up and turned to Robert and Charlie. "He says you are to return right away."

They rode in stony silence back to the office. Robert worked on keeping his temper in check, while trying to figure out how Crazy Charlie beat him to the house. With her on that wreck of a bike, it should have been a cakewalk for him. Maybe it had been the two minute delay for the train? Still, how had she made such good time with those big balloon tires and no gears?

Mr. Crabtree was waiting when they arrived.

"This is not the result I had expected. The thing is, I need a delivery boy, ah, girl. Dang it, I need *someone* to deliver the blasted telegrams!" The cigar rolled from one side of his mouth to the other, like a dead fish in the bottom of a boat.

Robert touched his pendant, the meteorite responding with a burst of warmth.

"You have to understand, kids, this is an auxiliary office, not the busiest by far for deliveries. If you two are willing to share the glory..." Here the telegrapher guffawed, "And the wages, I guess I could try you both out for now. No promises, mind you. Mrs. Crabtree thinks it would be ground breaking for me to employ a female as a delivery boy, I mean girl. Usually girls go for a telegrapher's job, operating one of those fancy Vibroplex bugs." He sized Charlie up. "I think I've got a uniform that will fit, almost."

The cigar made its way back to the other side of his mouth. "Now, down to brass tacks. You'll be paid three cents per delivery with a bonus of twenty five cents for Mewata and $2.50 for Bowness or Ogden due to sheer distance, as they're on the outskirts of town. I expect you to show up on time, be polite to customers and to keep your uniforms clean. You're representing CPR Telegraphs."

He disappeared into the back recesses while Robert and Charlie fumed at each other.

"You heard him," Charlie hissed. "At three cents each, it's going to take a lot of telegrams before I'm rolling in the dough and now I'll have to split the gold with you!"

Robert was not happy either, simply as a matter of principal. Crazy Charlie Donnelly should not be rewarded for being Crazy Charlie Donnelly. First the savings stamps, then the water tower, then the miraculous telegram delivery (he still didn't know how she'd pulled it off) and now she'd stolen half his income by taking a job no girl had a right to! Still, at three cents each, if he could deliver four telegrams a day, he'd have enough to buy his heroes and more! His brothers would be safe and he'd have all the comic books he wanted.

He supposed he could be generous. Maybe she wanted to buy something special, something unusual for her – like a dress.

"Stop bellyaching, Charlie. We're both stuck with the arrangement, unless you want to pull out..."

"As if!" she scoffed. "Why don't you scram? I was here first and I got to old lady Crabtree's house ahead of you. If anybody deserts it should be you, *Wonder Weed.*"

There was that rotten nickname again. He tried not to show how ticked off he was. It would give her his Achilles heel.

Mr. Crabtree walked out of the back carrying two charcoal grey uniforms, each with a peaked cap, pants like riding breeches, plus a tailored coat with shiny silver buttons. The CPR Telegraphs insignia was on the cap and collar. "It's a good thing you're a long drink of water, Miss Donnelly. The last boy who wore this was about your height." He issued each of them their uniforms and a handbook. "Read the regulations. Follow the procedures. New hires have two weeks to see if they're suited to the job, then I decide who stays. I'll expect you both here tomorrow after school and ready to roll."

As they left in sullen silence, Robert heard the staccato tapping of an outgoing message being keyed.

He watched Charlie wrestle with her heavy bicycle. "Where'd you get your pet dinosaur, anyway?"

She gave the bike a mighty heave and it came reluctantly loose from the rack. "I bought it on the weekend."

He laughed. "Bought it! Man, someone saw you coming."

She turned on him, hot anger spilling out. "Yeah, well if I hadn't worked my butt off to win the grease contest, I wouldn't even have this. I knew this job was coming up two weeks ago and made plans to make sure I got it. Then you waltz in here at the last minute, like some Johnny-come-lately, and try to shove me out! Well, you can think again," she smirked wickedly, "*Wonder Weed.*" Scrunching her uniform into her backpack, she leapt onto her old bike, straightened and peddaled away.

Robert watched her go. Trying to hide his dislike of the nickname didn't seem to have worked. "Shake it off, Tourond." He chided himself. "You can't let her get to you."

She'd made plans, had she? He remembered the smudged window with the job application sign and realized what had been on the glass. It hadn't been dirt, it had been *soap!* She'd tried to limit the number of applicants by hiding the blasted sign. And she'd wanted the stamps to trade in for cash, too!

Unbelievably, to buy that hunk of junk she rode. He didn't care what she'd done to get the job or why she wanted it so badly. He had a shot at earning enough money to make sure he got his comics, and if it meant riding over Charlie Donnelly, he had no problem. This was war and he took no prisoners!

CHAPTER THIRTEEN

FIRST BLOOD

ROBERT READ THE ADDRESS on his first delivery. He was pretty sure he knew where he had to go, but had taken the precaution of tucking a city map inside the pocket of his uniform jacket. He'd check to make sure he was right once he was a little further away. No sense in making the boss worry about the competency of his new delivery boy.

He had to admit, he was excited. His bike against Crazy Charlie's old junker-clunker was no contest. And when Mr. Crabtree assessed their work in two weeks, his lightning-speed deliveries may persuade the telegrapher that one super delivery *boy* was all he needed.

Crazy Charlie was also scrutinizing her first assignment. "Cakewalk," she said casually as she tucked the envelope into her satchel and turned for the door. Robert hurried after her.

"Where you off to?" he asked, eyeing her dilapidated bike. He wondered if Mr. Crabtree would give her addresses close by because Robert, with his superior set of wheels, stood less chance of breaking down.

"Across the Bow River."

Robert noticed she had her going-into-battle thing going again, thin lips and all.

"I'll be back in thirty."

"Sure you will," Robert hooted, knowing it was a long trip. "If you sprout wings and fly. I'm off to the Grain Exchange. Shouldn't be more than fifteen minutes round trip."

As Charlie peddaled off, Robert absently tapped his pendant and added up how much money he'd make if he were lucky enough to have all his deliveries come in at fifteen minutes per trip. He'd never miss another comic book again. The stone answered with a low-level vibration.

After a couple of false starts, Robert finally stood at the Grain Exchange receptionist's desk, cap set at a jaunty angle, buttons gleaming, the insignias plain for all to see. "CPR Telegraphs. Sign here, please, ma'am." He offered his Proof of Delivery book, an essential tool of his new trade.

With only the merest squint at the page, the receptionist scribbled her name and took the proffered telegram, which Robert had at the ready – a model of delivery-boy efficiency.

Within minutes, he was on his way back, his first three cents assured. He was whistling when he pulled up to the bicycle stand. Then he cursed with irritation: Crazy Charlie's beat-up wreck was already in the rack. Impossible! Hurrying inside, he caught the tail end of the conversation.

"This one goes to Bowness, a real trek, so you'll receive the big bonus."

Mr. Crabtree slid the telegram across the counter to Charlie.

Robert fumed. How had she done it? How had she made the round trip across the river in such a short space of time? That bonus job would have been his if he'd beaten her back. He should be the one getting an extra two-and-a-half dollars pay.

Swallowing his anger, Robert sat at the table in the corner designated *Staff,* and proceeded to wait...and wait, *and wait.* Lots of people came in with outgoing messages which the telegrapher added to his pile in the back room, but nothing for him. He remembered Mr. Crabtree saying the office wasn't the busiest for deliveries, no kidding, and they would be split between him and Charlie. If this was what it was going to be like, it would be darn hard to make enough to keep him in comic books.

Finally, after an ice age, Mr. Crabtree called him to the counter. "Tourond, you're off to the Grain Exchange Building again." "You bet, Mr. Crabtree." Robert accepted the telegram, and started back to his previous destination and the three cents it would earn.

He remembered thinking how great it would be to have a lot of fifteen minute deliveries. "Be careful what you wish for," he grumbled as he took off down the street.

By the time his shift was coming to a close, he had made only three deliveries: nine whole cents. It wasn't enough for one comic, let alone the army he had planned on buying. Still, if he averaged three a day, it added up to forty-five cents a week, a tidy sum that would buy him his three top heroes and a few new friends to join his cadre. Plus, some leftover change could go into the savings-stamp kitty, keeping his mother happy.

Charlie was still not back from her high-paying trip, but Bowness had a lot of topography. Without gears, it would be a tough, slow slog.

Because of the distance, Mr. Crabtree had said Charlie would be gone for the rest of the day, so when she walked in at quitting time, the surprise on his face was almost comical.

"Well now, I hadn't expected to see you again today. It's mighty impressive of you to come all the way back here, Donnelly." Mr. Crabtree rolled his unlit cigar around in his mouth.

Robert could see Charlie had sweated a lot in her uniform and her hair, which she'd braided into a long ponytail, had scraggly strands plastered to her neck.

"I thought you might need the log," she held the *Proof of Delivery* book out to him.

The telegraph operator took the book and nodded. "True enough. However, your employment forms say you live in Bowness, which is why I made it clear you could finish up the paperwork tomorrow."

Robert's mouth dropped open at this news. Bowness! It was nowhere near Crescent Heights. He lived in Pleasant Heights, the next district over, and even with that close proximity, he'd had a hard time getting into Crescent Heights High. What was she doing at their school if she lived out in Bowness?

Charlie was like a cornered animal, darting furtive glances at him as she tried to come up with an answer. "Yes, sir, I do live there. You should also know that my motto is 'the job comes first'."

Robert had to admit, he sure as heck wouldn't have come all the way back downtown from Bowness if he didn't have to. Crazy Charlie had lived up to her name again.

He was fussing with his bike when she emerged from the building. His delivery bag was in the basket and he rummaged in it pulling out the hip flask Patrick had loaned him. He was about to take a long swig, then noticed Charlie eyeing the bottle.

"It's only water," he said defensively. Robert remembered seeing her hand tremble when she'd turned in her log book and suspected she must be terribly thirsty from the long ride. "You want a drink?"

Charlie hesitated, as if about to say no, then nodded. "Thanks." Taking the bottle, she greedily tipped it up.

When she returned it, there wasn't a drop left. Robert took the empty flask and stashed it back in his bag, his own thirst unslaked. "Next time, bring water." He eyed her curiously. Even after the drink, she was a mess. "So why do you go to Crescent Heights High? You must have to get up at a pretty disgusting hour every day."

"You won't say anything will you, Wonder Weed? If they find out I don't live in the area, I'll have to go to school in Bowness."

"You haven't answered the question." He thought she was being evasive and was even more curious now.

"Guess I'm a sucker for a nifty brick building." She took off her grey uniform jacket and carefully folded it before stashing it in her delivery bag. Pausing, she added, "And it's a better school, no gangs, knives or trouble with the cops."

Robert had heard how tough the Bowness neighbourhood was and could understand wanting out. He thought of the long ride and remembered that she used to run, even in the winter, and kind of admired Charlie for what she was doing. He motioned to her clunker. "You traded a whole book of savings stamps for this, huh?"

"Even with the stamps, I had to borrow some dough to buy it. It cost me ten bucks."

"Ten dollars! The bike ain't the only thing that took you for a ride." His mouth spoke before his brain engaged.

She was instantly cold as January. "Yeah. I guess the dealership was all out of fancy import jobs when I got there."

And with lips as thin as razor blades, Crazy Charlie hopped on her bike and started her long trek back to Bowness.

ROBERT WAS LATE coming home, but his parents were thrilled when he told them about the job.

"I knew you were a Tourond through and through," his father said as Robert ate his warmed-over supper. "We've always been the type to take the bit in our mouths and run with it. This is a good introduction to the working world."

Robert was surprised. Usually his father said very little about the daily goings on of the family home, and when he did get chatty, it had nothing to do with praise.

"And it ties in nicely with the conversation we had about responsibility," his mother added, pouring Robert a cup of tea. "You'll be able to buy lots of stamps for your war savings certificates with the money."

Robert had feared his mother would head into that no-man's land. "I *will* buy stamps, Mum, I promise. I also want some of the money for my own, to spend on whatever I want."

"I suppose you mean those silly comic books?" Her clipped tone was filled with disapproval.

"Now, now, Helen," his father interjected. "I think the boy has a right to enjoy some of the gravy from his first real job. It will add to the experience of dealing with money and budgeting."

His mother thought this over. "I guess you're right. It's all part of growing up. I simply don't want him squandering his earnings."

"Have some faith." William Tourond said calmly. "He's a good head on his shoulders."

Again, Robert was thoroughly shocked at his father's support. He could have sworn his dad winked at him. Maybe it was a trick of the light.

CHAPTER FOURTEEN

ENEMY LINES

EVERY HOUR RACED BY in a blur – school all day, delivering telegrams until seven o'clock each night, a late dinner, homework, reading one of his heroes' adventures, then falling into bed to do it all again in the morning. It gave him a new appreciation for the stiffs who did it day in and day out for years.

Charlie turned out to be some kind of speed demon when it came to delivering telegrams. No matter how hard Robert pushed, she was always ahead of him, and on her dilapidated wreck, it should have been impossible. He had to find out her secret.

"You're having a good week," he commented casually as they collected their next deliveries. He couldn't help smiling, "As long as Big Betsy keeps rolling...I've noticed your times are really short and I was wondering how you –"

"Maybe you shouldn't spend so much of *your* time reading those," she interrupted, jutting her chin at the two comic books on the messenger table in the corner.

Robert had planned to reread Ice and the Kid on his break, but the delivery had interrupted this plan. He hastily picked up his telegram and ran to his bike, but Charlie was faster.

"See ya, Wonder Weed!" And before he could even climb onto the seat, she sped off.

He'd seen part of the address on her telegram and when he checked his own, noted both deliveries were in the same area. Robert decided to go as fast as possible, then follow Charlie and try to discover the secret to her speed.

He pushed off after her and churned as hard as he could. Up ahead, he could see her weaving in and out of traffic, splitting lanes and running reds. He wondered what Mr. Crabtree would say if he knew about all the traffic infractions Charlie racked up while in uniform. It was not the best advertising for CPR Telegraphs.

Then he thought of how often he bent the rules of the road if it meant getting the job done a few minutes faster. Maybe ratting on Charlie wasn't a good idea.

Up ahead, he saw the Forsyth Building, his destination, and wheeled onto the sidewalk.

Running into the building, he practically shoved the delivery book under the receptionist's nose. "Telegram. Sign here." She hadn't quite finished signing when Robert snatched the book, slapped the telegram on the counter and fled.

"Well, I never..." trailed after him as he raced for his bike.

Charlie had been going south on First Street and he knew she was on her way to Stephen Avenue. A delivery on such a busy road meant he'd have to dodge traffic while he scouted for Big Betsy in front of buildings, plus in the alleys and side streets. He'd also have to try and stay out of sight. If Charlie spotted him, she'd know he was following her to discover her secrets and he doubted she'd take kindly to his snooping.

Keeping his eyes peeled, he finally saw Charlie going into the Bank of Nova Scotia and swerved into an adjacent alley to wait. She had come out and was getting on her bike when Robert's view was blocked.

"Young man, I say, young man!" A stout woman in a brown coat and an extremely large flowered hat stood in front of him.

In case Robert hadn't heard her, she stepped even closer, effectively ending any hope of catching a glimpse of which direction Charlie took. Sometimes being in a uniform had its drawbacks. Telling the dame to back off was his first impulse; instead, he forced himself to be polite.

"Yes, ma'am. How can I help you?" Robert tried unsuccessfully to spot his competitor.

"I must send a telegram to my brother in Toronto. It's your job." She gave him an accusatory glare, daring him to contradict her.

She was kidding right? Was he supposed to magically whip a key out of his pocket and tap out a message?

"You'll have to go to the CPR Telegraphs office, ma'am. The address is 313-8th Avenue. I'm sure Mr. Crabtree would be happy to send your message."

She managed to be disgruntled, peeved and insulted all at the same time. "Traipse way down there? What a dreadful bother." She straightened her hideous hat like a knight adjusting his helmet before a joust. "Very well. If I must, I must. I'm not happy about this, young man." She strode off grumbling about "poor service." and muttering "what's the world coming to?"

Robert scanned the street. His nemesis had disappeared like a will o' the wisp, taking her secret with her. Wham! Kablam!

He started back to the telegraph office feeling tired and dejected. He was working harder than he ever had, but what with having to split deliveries and not getting very many high-paying runs, he wasn't rolling in dough like he thought he'd be. His dream of having all the comic books he wanted wasn't likely to happen. Plus, Robert knew his mum, who had such grand plans for his money, would want a big chunk of his pay when he brought it home. It wasn't fair. The more he thought about it, the angrier he felt.

At that moment, he passed Kreller's store. He deserved some reward for all his hard work and having to put up with Crazy Charlie. Robert knew exactly the reward he wanted. Turning his bike around, he rode down the sidewalk and parked in front of the store. Now that he had a respectable, bona fide job, he might be able to convince Mr. Kreller to advance him an issue of Canada Jack, with the promise he'd pay tomorrow.

Straightening his cap, Robert marched inside.

By the time he returned, Charlie Donnelly was already sitting at the messenger table, waiting. She watched him walk over.

"What kept you, Wonder Weed? Got lost or did you run out of pedal power?"

He was about to snap back at her when he saw what she was reading. It was his copy of *The Maple Leaf Kid*. Foolishly, he'd left his comic book on the table when he'd been called for his last delivery.

"Hey, give him back!" He reached for the comic.

With the reflexes of a cat – a polecat – Crazy Charlie snatched it away.

"You know, if you can make it past the main character's hokey movie star looks, and the unrealistic storyline, these aren't bad. In a juvenile sort of way."

He wasn't sure if he should be insulted or not. Since he and the Kid had a similar appearance, he liked the movie star reference. But he didn't much appreciate the "juvenile" crack. "You need to know the backstory of the characters and the plotlines already explored to truly appreciate the complexity of the overarching narrative." He'd used every ten cent word he could think of and, if he was asked to explain what he'd said, he'd be flummoxed. He hoped it sounded fancy enough to shut her up.

Charlie hesitated and Robert figured she was trying to unravel what he'd said.

"Nice to know you think the Kid's kinda handsome." With a theatrical flourish, he ran his fingers through his hair, which was, thankfully, starting to grow again.

She looked up, then at the page, and then quickly back at him.

"I guess, in a homely sort of way...like the ugly-duckling cousin you feel sorry for," she teased.

What happened next was close to a miracle.

Crazy Charlie Donnelly *smiled*.

It made her face light up, like a ray of sunshine blazing through a dark thunderhead. It was so unexpected and rare, it threw him off balance. The sharp remark he'd been about to hurl at her for taking his comic evaporated and, much to his amazement, he didn't feel like coming up with a new one.

"Didn't the ugly duckling turn out to be a handsome prince in the end?" he quipped instead.

Charlie started to pull her lips into the well-known and oft-used battle line expression. Instantly, Robert steeled himself for a fight, and then they both realized it was too late. The tension in the room had boiled off.

"*Swan*, a handsome *swan*, which is still a birdbrain, Wonder Weed." Carefully closing the comic, she pushed it across the table. "I have to admit, it was pretty good."

"Feel free to borrow my quality literature any time you want." He went to the hot plate and the coffee pot Mr. Crabtree kept perennially simmering. "Want a cup of joe?" he asked in his best telegram delivery *man* accent, affecting an air of maturity he hoped he could pull off.

Her brow arched. "Joe, no, a cup of *Josephine*, yes." Then she added, "Please." Robert poured them each a cup, and they took a sip of the black brew, then grimaced.

"Wow, did this come out of some old car crankcase?" Charlie choked.

"More like the La Brea Tar Pits." Robert coughed. "Maybe more milk...and definitely more sugar."

They both doctored their coffees, then Charlie took a tentative sip. "Better, still not good. I wonder if I should worry about it eating away my stomach."

They sat in companionable silence sipping their strong brews and then Mr. Crabtree interrupted with another telegram.

"Last delivery for today, fellas...tarnation, I mean, *people*," he corrected himself. "Technically, it should be yours, Donnelly, since you were first back. Thing is, it's close to Tourond's house, which is in the wrong direction for you. We're only talking three cents here, want to give it to him?"

"No sir. I'll take it." Abruptly, she stood and buttoned her collar, then yanked down on her jacket to straighten it.

It was as if the camaraderie they'd shared a moment before never happened. Charlie's mouth became a thin red line and Robert knew the barbed wire fence was back.

She took the telegram and as she left, he thought he saw a shadow of something cross her face. Exhaustion?

CHAPTER FIFTEEN

COMIC BOOK KING

THE NEXT DAY DRAGGED by so painfully, Robert wondered if he was in an altered, slow motion universe. The only thing that kept him going was the pot of gold at the end of the rainbow – his first pay, due this very night at quitting time.

Waiting impatiently at the staff table, Robert already knew exactly what he would do with his money. It was all he'd thought about. His first stop would be Kreller's Drugstore. Thanks to his inheriting more of the Tourond silver tongue than he'd thought, he'd been able to convince the pharmacist to give him Canada Jack early. It had been worth it, but Mr. Kreller had been very reluctant, frosty even, and Robert knew he'd probably used up all the goodwill the shop owner had for him. Maybe clearing his debt promptly would help get Robert back into Mr. Kreller's good graces. And then – and this was the good part – then he would buy whatever comic book hero he wanted, no matter how extravagant or exotic. He'd had four deliveries this shift, his best day ever, and was expecting thirty-six cents hard cash in total.

Finally, his boss walked over to the table with two envelopes. "Good job, folks."

"Thank you, Mr. Crabtree." Robert stood to take the pay packet and had the weird urge to salute. He noticed Charlie's envelope was fatter than his. Maybe next week, he'd get a long haul, high-paying delivery to even the score.

"So, what are you going to do with your big payday?" he asked Charlie as they left work. "Buy something wild and frivolous for yourself?"

She gave him a glower that made him wince and wither.

"Or maybe not..." he added.

"It's *maybe not*, for me." She leaned against her bike and opened her envelope, inspecting the contents. "Seems like a lot of work for this. Though, I shouldn't complain. Any money is good money and it's more than I had a week ago."

Robert figured if she could count her gold, so could he, and he ripped open the end of his envelope. Pouring the coins into his hand, he scowled.

"Wham! Kablam! This can't be right." He counted the money again. Twenty-four cents! By his reckoning, he was short twelve cents.

Charlie tucked her envelope into her delivery bag. "Not the big score you were expecting?"

"I'm sure there should be another twelve cents in here."

She gazed into his palm, like a gypsy reading his fortune, or lack of it. "Nope. Looks right. Like you, I've been keeping score." Then understanding lit her face. "I bet you forgot Crabtree was keeping back today's wages. He said he holds Friday's in case there's any problems, or if he needs to change something. If everything's okay, it will be in next week's pay packet."

Robert remembered Mr. Crabtree had told them about this procedure. In the excitement of being hired, he'd missed some of the details. "Right...I forgot. I owe some money to someone and this won't leave me much."

Charlie's lips slid into their usual hard line. "Been there, but I'd never have pegged you for having troubles like that, Wonder Weed. It's more something you'd hear about from my side of the tracks."

He must have come across as truly anxious, because Charlie stopped her needling. "Hey, if you're short, Rob, I can lend you some until next week."

He thought she was being sarcastic, and then he studied her face and saw she was serious. He hadn't expected this. "Ah, no, I'm okay." He tucked the money into his trouser pocket, then tipped his head at her quizzically. "*Rob*, huh?"

She punched him on the shoulder, hard. "Don't get any ideas, Wonder Weed. We're still mortal enemies. When Crabtree gives us his review next week and says he's keeping me because I'm so efficient and skidding you, then don't expect any goodbye party."

The thought of losing even this meagre money was scary, and Robert unconsciously touched the pendant under his grey jacket. "And if he comes to his senses and decides a *man* is better for the job, then you'll get the same lack of consideration from me."

Their words would have sounded tougher if they hadn't been smiling.

She hit him again, not as hard this time. "Buck up. It's Friday night, no work for the weekend, and we have money, even if it's only a little, in our dungarees." Struggling, she wrestled her heavy bike out of the rack. "And, like you, I need every red cent I can get. It's my only shot."

This she said as much to herself as to him and Robert wondered what she meant. They parted ways but when he checked in her direction, he saw her watching him. Charlie's offer of a loan had been unexpected and he wasn't sure he would have done the same. Without thinking, he raised his arm and waved. Crazy Charlie didn't wave back.

DESPITE NOT HAVING the vast fortune he'd hoped for, Robert couldn't help feeling elated as he rode to Kreller's Drugstore. He could pay for the comic he'd taken on credit, and still have enough left over to buy another if he wanted, and he wanted. It wouldn't leave much for his mother's savings-stamp fund, but he deserved it and he'd make up the shortfall next week when he'd be rolling in the dough.

"Hey, Mr. Kreller. I'm here to pay for Canada Jack and I believe I'll take this copy of *Nelvana of the Northern Lights* as well." He held up the new comic as he casually slid the money across the counter.

The old pharmacist was still cool toward Robert, giving him a curt nod. "Nice to have such a good *cash-paying* customer."

"This is only the beginning, Mr. Kreller. I'm going to be your best customer."

Robert rode home pleased with himself, the weekend stretching ahead, along with the promise of more money and more comics next week.

"THIS IS ALL YOU MADE?" his mother exclaimed when he laid the four cents on the table at supper.

"Actually, it was a short week and I have to split the deliveries with another messenger plus Mr. Crabtree holds back one day's pay. There'll be more next week." Robert listed his acceptable excuses, knowing he couldn't tell his mother about paying for one comic and buying another.

"Still, it's not reasonable pay for three day's work, son," his father added as he spooned his meatless spaghetti sauce over the noodles.

Robert figured he'd better 'fess up, at least to part of it. "I also owed money to someone and wanted to clear the slate."

This got both his parents' attention.

"You owed money!" His mother's tone was shrill.

TOO LATE, OUR HERO SAW HIS FATAL ERROR! HE AND THE ENEMY BOTH KNEW THE RULES OF COMBAT. HE'D LET HIMSELF SLIP AND NOW HIS MISSION WAS IN JEOPARDY!

"Not a lot. I remembered what you taught me and decided I should pay my debts before anything else. It was the honourable thing to do." Robert hoped this would appeal to her sense of justice and ethics and, after all, it was the truth. He'd paid Mr. Kreller for Canada Jack before buying another comic.

Unexpectedly, his father spoke up in his defence. "Robert's right. It was the honourable thing to do, Helen. I wouldn't have expected anything less of the boy."

"After all, Mum, you always say, 'Owe the Lord, not thy neighbour'." He'd never heard her say anything of the kind, but it sounded good now.

His mother wasn't that easy to sidetrack. "What I say, young man, is, 'Neither a borrower nor a lender be'." She fussed with the biscuit bowl, rearranging the napkin covering the steaming buns. "I wanted to be able to tell my Knit for Victory group all about Robert's job and the savings stamps and certificates he's buying. I guess I can wait until next week when he can make up for this, this..." she waved at the four copper pennies sitting forlornly on the table, "...humble start."

Then she sighed, loud and long. "I made you this." She reached under the table and withdrew a quart sealer jar. "It's like a piggy bank."

His mother had glued strips of a victory poster around the jar, and Robert could see the cartoon lion of England, complete with crown, beside the Canadian beaver, with sword and helmet, charging against the enemy. The caption read, *To Victory*.

"And there's more." She again reached under the table, this time retrieving a poster of a sailor, out of uniform, on the deck of a ship and holding a shell. The caption read:

How quickly can we complete his outfit?

Every war savings stamp helps speed victory.

"Each stamp buys another part of his uniform and when you're done, there's a tiny bomber plane we get to add to my poster map in the basement. We can buy an entire squadron to help defeat *that Hitler*."

His mother was on a roll now, and Robert wondered what was next. As if on cue, she pulled another poster from the seemingly inexhaustible supply of gifts hiding under the dining room table.

"I thought this picture was like one of your comic book

characters, and I liked the encouraging message." She stood and held up the poster. It featured a fresh-faced, red-headed boy calling to his imagined friends: *Hey gang! Keep on licking war savings stamps – they're full of vitamin "V."*

His mother wasn't exactly subtle and Robert began to wonder what the heck she had set up in the basement. Was it some sort of secret bunker where Canadian mothers made plans to defeat the Axis by knitting bombs and forcing their kids to buy twenty-five cent savings stamps?

Robert decided he needed to be very careful about how much information he gave his mum on the number of telegrams he delivered, where he delivered them or anything else which might give a clue to his expected wages.

Loose lips sink ships. Or, in his case, *loose lips cost comics.*

Later Robert set to work on his own victory project. He'd retrieved all the copies of *Sedna of the Sea*, *Captain Ice* and *The Maple Leaf Kid* he had collected, and arranged them on his dresser in neat stacks next to the appropriate brother's picture. He then moved his floor lamp over and angled the shade so the light shone down on his artfully arranged display. Once he was satisfied at the effect, he stepped back and saluted, taking off his lucky charm. He felt a tingle when he touched his talisman.

"Everyone agrees the best course of action is to give Mum as little information as possible." Then, eyeing the copies of *Canada Jack* and *Nelvana of the Northern Lights*, he added a little guiltily, "And perhaps, I won't buy other comic books and will stick to you top three for now. It's only logical to ensure the success of our mission, especially if I'm expected to supply squadrons of paper planes."

Robert could have sworn he heard a murmur of agreement and felt better as he settled in to read his new adventure. When he was ready for sleep, he decided that, from now on, the spotlight would be left burning to illuminate his display. Then, if he woke in the night, the first thing he would see was his heroes, all six of them.

CHAPTER SIXTEEN

BAD WEEK

As Robert passed Mr. G's on his way to school Monday, he waved cheerily. *"Witaj i Żegnaj!"* He sang out, knowing his pronunciation was mangled, but doing his best. He'd asked one of his Polish customers how to say "hello and goodbye" with the result being both words threaded together as a phrase which, Robert guessed, covered all bases. He'd been dying to show off his new words.

"*Doskonałe*, excellent, Robcio!" his neighbour called back. "How problem with young lady coming along?"

"Nothing I can't handle!" Robert yelled over his shoulder.

He had his uniform in his bike basket and would change into it at work instead of coming home as he had been. When Crazy Charlie arrived, he'd be there, suited up and raring to go, or even better, already on his first delivery. She'd continued to annoy him with times no one should be able to pull down on a wreck like hers.

His master plan was torpedoed out of the water when he wheeled up to the office and saw Big Betsy in the rack. It sported a spiffy new wicker basket, which was completely out of place on the beat-up old cruiser.

"Hey, Wonder Weed." Charlie came out of the washroom at the back of the office as he walked in. She was in full uniform and stuffing her street clothes into her backpack. "I got caught trying to change in the park on the way here, so I decided to play it safe. I see you had the same idea." She motioned to the uniform in his arms.

"Ah, yeah. I mean, no. I didn't get caught in the park." Frustration gnawed at his gut. Charlie Donnelly was the most aggravating, sneaky, underhanded...

"If you didn't get caught, why are you still in your civvies?"

"Oh, I didn't mean I was putting my uniform on in the park, I meant, I had the same idea, to change. Here, I mean..." His tongue was having trouble forming words that wouldn't make him sound like an idiot.

"I hope you straightened things out with the loan shark you owed." She tossed her bag onto the small, worn settee near the table. The couch was so old, the horsehair stuffing was sticking out from the small holes scattered in it like a shotgun blast.

At first, Robert couldn't figure out what she was talking about and then he remembered his pay shortage on Friday. "No worries there. Debt's cleared." This was true. He'd paid the pharmacist.

"Good stuff. Some jerks you never want to mess with. Take the knee-breakers in my neighbourhood; they'd have made short work of a nice guy like you."

"Telegrams for delivery and I need the pair of you, *now!*" Mr. Crabtree boomed from the back room, and Robert and Charlie both jumped.

"Hurry up!" Charlie whispered. "Get your uniform on! I'll stall."

Robert was confused. Crazy Charlie Donnelly, who thought nothing of blasting you out of the sky if she had the chance, was going to cover for him? But why? Getting him into trouble with the boss would fit right into her nasty plans. He ran for the washroom, fumbling with the buttons on his shirt.

Straightening his jacket, Robert raced to the counter, just as Mr. Crabtree emerged from his office.

"Where's Donnelly? I thought she was already here."

Charlie came to stand behind Robert.

"I'm here, Mr. Crabtree." She piped up brightly.

The telegrapher was particularly irritable as he chewed on his unlit cigar. Robert wondered if it was the same one or if the old codger eventually worried the stogies to bits and replaced them with new ones.

Mr. Crabtree held up two telegrams. "They're a ways out, but neither is in the "bonus zone," which means they're still three-centers. Even so, no smart mouths with these, understand? Respect. I also want you to stay to make sure the addressee is okay and go get a neighbour if they seem unsteady and no one's home."

Robert was taken aback. What was this all about? He slid a peek at Charlie, who was listening intently with her usual going-to-war face resolutely in place.

Once outside, Charlie fiddled with her big bike. "You know what these are, don't you?"

"Yup. Three cents in my pocket," he answered as he retrieved his own faster and lighter three-speed.

"No, Wonder Weed, they're *military* telegrams. We've got to deliver the news that someone's son or husband is missing in action or, worse, dead. I knew this would be part of the job, but I have to tell you, it kinda spooks me."

Robert hadn't thought of this aspect. "Well, sure, delivering bad news is tragic business. You have to keep in mind, that's exactly what it is – business. If I worried about what was in every telegram, I couldn't work here. What if it's news some guy's company has failed and he's wiped out? What about medical results for some schmuck letting him know the undertaker is headed his way? Nope, I can't get personal."

He tucked his telegram in his pouch. "I'm going to Erlton, where's yours?"

"Holy Cross Hospital. This poor sod is sick and now I've got to bring more rotten news." She dusted off the insignia on her collar. "I hope they don't shoot the messenger." She swung her leg over the bar of her bike. "See ya."

"Yeah, see ya." He watched her as she left. This side of Crazy

Charlie was new – it was almost human.

The bike ride to Erlton went smoothly enough and within minutes he was at the house. His knock was answered by a woman who took one look at his uniform, then blanched as white as paste. She stood in the doorway, not moving. "Ah, telegram for Mrs. Tom Borch." She remained a pale statue. He tried again. "Is that you, ma'am?" This time the woman slowly nodded her head.

Robert held the Proof of Delivery book out to her. "Sign here, please." He indicated the space next to her name. She took the pen he offered and scribbled something illegible.

He relinquished the telegram, only then noticing she was shaking. Without a word, she turned away and closed the door in his face.

"Another satisfied customer," he mumbled under his breath and hurried back out to his bike.

By the time Charlie returned to the office, Robert had made two more deliveries and was mentally adding up his wages for the week.

"What took you so long? Did Big Betsy spring a leak in those fatso tires?" he teased as she walked in and sat at their table. "Or maybe *you* got lost."

"Actually, the telegram turned out to be for one of the Grey Nuns who nurse at the hospital. I took her back to the Nun House, or whatever it's called, so she could be with the other sisters." Charlie flopped down into a wooden armchair. "She was pretty upset and I didn't want her to be alone."

"While you were off playing Florence Nightingale, it was left to me to cover deliveries. Fortunately, I was up to the task and completed two more," Robert boasted. He was about to add another scathing comment, when he saw her face. It was etched bone-deep with fatigue.

Mr. Crabtree came out of the back room, interrupting their conversation. "How'd it go, folks?"

"Fine, sir," Charlie said in a small voice as she stood, pulling down on her jacket.

"Usually I deliver the bad ones, but since my other telegrapher joined up for service, I can't get away from the blasted key. I know it's a tough part of the job, Donnelly." His voice held more than a little sympathy.

Robert didn't say anything.

THE NEXT DAY WAS the same, and the next. It was as if the army had opened its roster of military personnel and sent a flood of bad news to the families of everyone listed. There were a lot of telegrams – lots of bad news, but good for Robert's pay packet.

On one particularly rushed day, it was Charlie's turn for the next delivery, but when the call came, she instantly busied herself with her tea. "Rob, I can't face another of those, those...*death notices* right now. Would you mind taking this one?"

He sat up in surprise. Charlie giving him a delivery? Now, this was new.

"Sure, no problem." He went to the counter, and if Mr. Crabtree noticed, he made no comment as he slid Robert the telegram.

"You know the drill, son."

Even the crusty old telegrapher sounded worn out to Robert.

He raced to the address, hoping if he hurried, he could get in three or four more deliveries today. He could really use a big score. The October editions of his buddies were due in soon and he needed money.

Leaning his bike against a white picket fence, Robert leaped up the porch steps, then rapped smartly on the door until a very pregnant young woman with a small child on her hip answered his summons.

"Can I help you?" she asked.

"Telegram for Mrs. Samuel Goldstein." He watched the colour drain out of her face as though a plug had been pulled.

"I'm Mrs. Goldstein." The young woman's voice had dropped to a whisper. She opened the door. "Come in. There's no reason the whole neighbourhood needs to know my business."

Robert stepped into the foyer of the tidy house. The woman

signed his delivery book and took the telegram. "Please, hold Rebecca." She unceremoniously dumped the child into Robert's arms.

Ripping the envelope open, she read it. "This must be wrong. My Abraham only left for overseas two weeks ago. I got a letter from him yesterday. Yes, it must be a mistake." Her eyes pleaded with Robert to agree, and then when he said nothing she carefully folded the letter and put it in her apron pocket.

She took the child back, her voice barely audible. "Thank you. I'd like to be alone now."

Her pale face and strange calmness made Robert nervous. "Would you like me to get a neighbour?"

"No, no." Her voice was oddly monotone, almost robotic. "The neighbours can't help me now."

Robert belatedly took his cap off as he slowly backed toward the door.

"If you're sure you're okay, I'd best be going." Glad to escape, he left, closing the door quietly behind him.

He'd made it down two steps when he heard an unearthly keening coming from behind the closed door. It was like a wounded animal caught in a trap with no way out. Robert had never heard a sound like that from another human being. It felt like ice crystals had formed in his blood and, despite the unseasonably warm weather, he was chilled. He couldn't leave her alone, no matter what she said.

As he made his way next door, it hit him how he and Charlie had delivered loads of these telegrams and they were only two in an army of messengers all over Canada. And what about the States and Britain and their delivery boys?

An older woman came to the door, wiping her hands on a dish towel. Robert had barely introduced himself and she was taking off her apron and house slippers and putting on her shoes. She thanked Robert for fetching her and hurried up Mrs. Goldstein's walk.

As Robert got back on his bike, he felt better. Then he recalled that earlier in the day, Mr. Crabtree had told them there must have been a big push *over there* in late September to account for the rush of telegrams. Robert remembered Patrick's letter about going into Italy and the heavy fighting expected. The thought made him queasy.

By FRIDAY, CHARLIE WAS frayed to unravelling and even Robert had started to feel the strain. He figured he'd seen it all: disbelief and shock, rejection and anger – or worse – humble acceptance, and then a terrible crumbling, like a sandcastle when the tide sweeps in. To get through it, Robert had a system where he would convince himself they weren't death notices he was delivering, only wounded or missing in action notifications.

At night, he'd talk to his squad of heroes, telling them about his day. If his mother noticed the arrangement on his dresser, with the three stacks of comic books and the spotlight shining on them and his brothers, she said nothing.

Friday's shift was finally, mercifully, coming to a close and Robert was glad. It had been an unbelievable week. Rolling back in from his last delivery, he arrived at the same time as Charlie. Her face was pale and pinched, and Robert wondered if the war telegrams were getting to her, too. "You okay?"

"What's it to you?" she said sharply

Robert felt like she'd slapped him. "Nothing. You look like death warmed over, no offence."

"Thanks for the compliment. You really know how to make a girl feel special."

They'd been getting along pretty well all week and this change in attitude, back to the truly nasty Crazy Charlie, was unexpected. Then he thought of how upset she'd been delivering her first death telegram to the nun and how many similar messages they'd had this week and decided to cut her some slack. He fell back on the salve he knew best. "You need a cup of tea. Come on, I'll make you one. None of the tar Crabtree brews in that cauldron he calls a coffee pot."

Charlie paused, wariness on her face, then she accepted his

offer as genuine. "Actually, tea would be swell."

They walked inside, and Charlie immediately went to the alcove where the staff table was and slumped down in a chair, then hunched over and hugged her stomach.

Robert put the kettle on the electric hot plate, and found the canister of tea leaves and a pot. "You're sure you're okay?"

Charlie groaned. "Don't tell Crabtree or he'll say I can't do my job. I'll be fine tomorrow."

So the telegrams were getting to her. He made the tea, then brought a cup and gingerly pushed it toward her from the far side of the table. Milk and sugar followed the teacup. "I understand, these things can really lay you low," he said sympathetically.

She stared at him in disbelief. "Oh, for crying out loud. It's a *girl thing*, Wonder Weed, not leprosy!" She started to giggle, then clutched her stomach again. "Augh!" she grimaced. "Don't make me laugh or I'll throw up for sure."

Was he missing something? "I'm sorry to say this, but you really are crazy, Charlie." He patted the pillow on the old couch. "At least come and sit here. It's more comfortable."

She stuck her tongue out at him, then brought her tea and eased herself down. Robert settled into rereading a copy of *The Maple Leaf Kid.* The Kid and his world made more sense than his own, right now. The drawings were more than ink lines on paper; sometimes, he could swear they moved. Robert gave a small nod to the Kid and the Kid waved back at him from his world.

When Mr. Crabtree walked over, Charlie and Robert were both quietly enjoying their own pursuits and sipping their tea.

"You two kids have worked hard this week; a real credit to the uniform. I have no complaints about either one. This has been an unusual week and, I must admit, I was very glad to have the both of you here."

In all the frantic hustle of the last few days, Robert had completely forgotten that today was when Mr. Crabtree would judge their performance and decide who stayed and who hit the road.

The portly telegrapher rolled the ever-present cigar back and forth and Robert tried to hide his smile. He'd figured out the secret of the unlit stogie when Mr. Crabtree had left the door to his office open one day and Robert happened to pass by at exactly the right moment. His boss didn't smoke: not cigars, not cigarettes, not a pipe. He did, however, keep a bottle of twelve-year-old Scotch in his desk drawer and would dip the end of the cigar in the bottle. Then he'd keep the booze-soaked Cuban special tucked in the corner of his mouth.

Robert couldn't help admiring the man's method. One, there was no foul odour of cigar smoke; two, there was no evidence of alcohol lying around, and three, Mr. Crabtree saved money on both cigars and Scotch, a detail sweet old Mrs. Crabtree was surely grateful for.

"I was worried I wouldn't have enough work for two messengers and neither of you would make a decent wage. After this week, I've changed my mind. I think everything evens out – it's either chicken or feathers in this business. When it's chicken, we all eat; if it's feathers, well now, you be glad your folks can step in to feed you." Mr. Crabtree chuckled, and this time he made a gurgling sound like muddy water going down a drain. "And if you two can be civil to one another while on the job," here he raised his unkempt brows at them, "I'm prepared to leave things as they are. You can both stay if you choose."

The comment about Charlie and him getting along surprised Robert. He didn't think the old guy had picked up on the hostility they felt for each other. Even though things had eased to a halfway truce, he'd have to be more careful in the future. If things did get too slow to support two couriers, then he didn't want to stick out as the one who couldn't get along with the rest of the team.

Robert took his pay envelope and hefted it. Hard work and the war were paying off. He'd have no problem buying all three of his heroes when they came in next week, and his mother would be thrilled as there would be enough to buy more saving stamps to add to his book.

"So, are we sticking together as a merry little band?" Mr. Crabtree asked.

Robert and Charlie fidgeted like kids at a prayer meeting.

"Rob's not so bad, once you get over his ugly mug smiling like a jack-in-the-box puppet all day," Charlie offered in way of agreement.

Robert added his two cents. "And Charlie's pile of rusty bolts keeps me entertained all shift. Her bike's pretty funny, too!" He added as a parting shot.

Mr. Crabtree made another of his gurgling sounds. "Then it's settled. Be here after school Monday. Now go, the pair of you." He turned and went back to the telegrapher's room.

Robert could have sworn he heard the sound of a cork being pulled.

CHAPTER SEVENTEEN

UNKNOWN WORLDS

ON THE WAY HOME, Robert felt his pendant humming – something big was about to happen. He knew better than to disregard the signal and decided to ride to his favourite drugstore to see if any of his top three buddies had arrived early. He'd barely walked into the shop, when Mr. Kreller called him over.

"Darndest thing, Robert, all three of your favourite comics came in today. They're a few days ahead of schedule, which is strange. If you want only one in particular, say *The Maple Leaf Kid*," he paused to let Robert think about his offer, "you can get it today."

Robert felt his pulse speed up. "I'll take..." He patted his trouser pocket, feeling the pay-packet money. "All three of them."

The pharmacist froze, obviously surprised at this grand order; then he pulled a paper bag from beneath the counter and loaded it up. "That'll be thirty cents, cash."

Robert extracted the money and took the bag. He could hardly contain his excitement. He had all three of his super-heroes' new releases at once! He couldn't remember that ever happening before.

What would the covers be like? What adventures awaited? What danger would Ice get into, and out of, this month? And Sedna, what watery mission would she and her fishy friends go on?

The best of the best would be discovering how the Kid, his special pal, had devised some ingenious plan to outsmart Hitler. What peril lurked for his buddy, and how would he thwart the evil mastermind?

It was all waiting for him.

Robert had the urge to drop everything and snoop in the bag. He couldn't, though. He knew if he saw so much as the corner of a cover, he would have to read the entire story then and there. After all, it was like having a window into what was happening to his brothers. He knew when their letters arrived the comic book world would already have shown him what had been happening to them.

Careering into the alley behind his house, he threw a fast wave to Mr. G, then stashed his bike in the garage, raced into the house and straight upstairs to his room. A quick salute to his brothers, then Robert leapt onto the bed and, taking his pendant out from under his shirt, held it as he reached into the brown bag and withdrew the prize.

"Who's the lucky winner in this month's comic book lottery? It's our old friend, Captain Ice. Congratulations..." Robert trailed off as he stared down at the cover. The image made his breath stop in his chest and he blinked. This couldn't be right. It was some kind of cosmic prank.

The cover showed George's guardian with blood trickling down the side of his battered face as he dangled from a parachute and watched his smoking plane spiral to the ground in flames. All around were fiery explosions from German anti-aircraft guns. Other planes were tied up in dogfights, the allies obviously losing the battle, as gleeful Nazi pilots sped by, wing-mounted machine guns blazing.

In the far distance, across the English Channel, were the white cliffs of Dover. Ice was coming down in France – *behind enemy lines.*

Stunned, Robert couldn't think straight. This had to be wrong; some mistake drawn by the artist. He checked the date. It was the latest edition alright. Panic swallowed him whole.

Shaking, he took the next comic book out of the bag. It was *Sedna of the Sea*. A pod of orcas surrounded James' guardian as she piloted a torpedoed supply ship safely into harbour. The sailors on the ship cheered, their lives saved by this daring aqua-heroine.

Next, Robert pulled *The Maple Leaf Kid* from the bag. Relief flooded through him as he took in the scene pictured. The Kid held plans for a portable bridge being assembled to help troops cross a wide river. Canadian tanks were lined up, ready to blast the retreating Nazis. There would be no rest for the enemy, thanks to the Maple Leaf Kid.

Captain Ice was the only comic showing a story with grim news. Maybe Robert was wrong and the comics didn't foretell what was coming. Maybe it was all a mistake...

He'd been holding his meteorite so tightly, his fingers ached. Out of the corner of his eye, he glimpsed his brothers' pictures lined up precisely on his dresser, the spotlight shining on their smiling faces.

"Don't get worried if I tell you I haven't a clue what's going on. I'm sure there's an explanation and everything will work out." Something occurred to him that he hadn't thought of before. "Hey, maybe the cover is picturing some nightmare Ice had, and it's not real. Of course! It must be the classic dream sequence."

Slipping his lucky charm over his head, Robert picked up the comic and, sitting on the edge of his bed, quickly read the entire story. He waited for everything to be explained, for Ice to wake up safely in his own bed at the aerodrome after a particularly gruelling, yet totally successful, mission over enemy territory.

As Robert read, the perilous fate of his hero Captain Ice was drawn plainly in black and white. Every detail was clear, from the cannon round slamming into Invincible over the English Channel, to the tracer bullets from the Nazi gunner who was trying to shoot Ice's parachute lines as he drifted toward the French coast, sending him plummeting to his death far below.

The scene was so real, Robert felt like he could reach into the page and touch the ace as he hung suspended in that deadly sky, waiting for fate to deal the cards. Robert said a silent prayer as he turned the page for the final scene.

The image took his breath away! It was wonderful, it was spectacular, it was salvation! Quickly, he took in the storyline. Ice had landed in a forest, and was met by a French Resistance squad, part of the Maquis. Under cover of darkness, they got him through enemy lines to the coast. From there he was smuggled aboard a ship bound for England. The last panel showed Ice on the deck, smiling back as a beautiful and voluptuous French freedom fighter in a beret waved goodbye, a shiny tear glistening on her cheek. Ice had done it again!

Robert had to read the other comics to see what was happening with their heroes. He'd need a block of undisturbed time, which meant going to his mother and giving her his wages. When she was all happy, he'd beg off supper. He could eat later and escaping the family meal would give him the much-needed time to concentrate on his friends' stories.

He hurried downstairs and then stopped at the murmur of voices coming from the living room. His parents must be there and not in the kitchen. Robert swerved toward the sound.

"Mum, I know you'll be thrilled when you see this week's pay packet –" He stopped when he saw the man in uniform sitting with his parents.

His mother, on the couch with his father, wrung the hanky she was holding. When she spoke, there was a quaver in her voice. "Robert, this is Squadron Leader Aberdeen. He's married to Susan, from my Knit for Victory Club. There's news about George and the squadron leader offered to come and personally tell us. So kind, when he's such a busy man."

Robert thought of all those telegrams he'd delivered this week, then addressed the squadron leader. "Is George back in England? Have you heard from the Maquis?"

His parents were startled at his questions. "What are you talking about, Robert?" his father asked.

Robert looked from one confused face to the next. "George...his plane was shot down over the English Channel, right?"

"Not quite; it was on the French coast. But how did you know?" The air officer stood, using a cane to steady himself.

"He must have overheard us talking." His mother turned to her friend's husband. "Who are these Maquis? If you know something Harold, you have to tell us."

Squadron Leader Aberdeen paused, thinking something over. "This is most unusual, highly irregular, but it seems the cat is already out of the bag. What I am about to tell you must remain in this room. Do you understand?"

They all nodded mutely.

"There is a chance George has been picked up by the Maquis, part of the French Resistance. Keep in mind; we don't know this for sure. Robert, I think you're guessing, or perhaps, hoping, this is what has happened to your brother. I must stress again, we have no confirmation. If I hear anything, I will contact you immediately."

"When," Robert corrected automatically. "*When* you hear, sir."

The squadron leader laid a gentle hand on Robert's shoulder. "I hope you're hunch is right, son."

After he left, Robert's mother sat silently, still clasping her hanky tightly in her lap. His father restlessly paced up and down the worn carpet.

"Don't worry. George is going to be okay. I know it." Robert tried to reassure his parents as best he could.

"How can you know, Robert, when even the military has no idea where he is or even if he's alive?"

"Oh, William, what if our boy is..." His mother's whispered sentence was never finished.

Robert again thought of the telegrams he'd delivered and the grief etched on the faces of the people receiving those messages of doom. He hated to see that same grief on his mother's face when it wasn't necessary. "Mum, he's fine..."

"Robert, I understand that you want your brother to be safe," his father said sympathetically. "We all want that. The truth is, you can't know anything more than we do."

Robert's frustration flared like a freshly lit match. "I do

know, Dad. It's hard to explain. You have to trust me." He was putting a lot of faith in his comic book connection, but he knew he was right.

"How can you be so sure?"

"It's a long story, Dad. I think it all started the night I found my meteorite. Wait a minute." Hurriedly, Robert went upstairs to get the comic books and his brothers' letters, and then he explained in as much detail as possible how he knew what was happening. "So, you see, the comic books and my letters are saying the same thing about what's going on over there. It's like reading the news before it's happened," he finished.

"I read those letters and there was nothing about mines and planes." His mother sounded confused.

Robert had the decency to look chagrined. "It's because we write in code, Mum. It's so no one can understand us and we can say things that would otherwise be cut out by the censors."

"And since I've not been told any of this, I guess I'm on your list of those who don't need to know what's in those letters?" In his mother's tone, Robert heard the sound of enemy engines revving up.

"No, mum, we did it so I could hear the boy stuff, stuff ladies would be bored hearing. You know how they are, always bragging."

His father interrupted him, "So you are telling us you think George is safe based on the strength of a ten-cent comic book?"

"I showed you how the stories and the guys' experiences were the same..."

"I think that's enough, Robert!" his father cut him off. "This has no basis in fact and it's upsetting your mother. I don't want to hear any more of this nonsense."

Nonsense? Robert was the one confused now. He'd shown his parents how it worked.

"You don't understand..." Robert started to explain again.

"No more talk like this." His father was as close to shouting as Robert had ever heard.

"Fine!" Robert felt his pendant beat against his chest like a drum. He was so angry; he had to get out of there before he said something he could never take back. "I'm going out. I'll be back later."

He picked up his comics and coat, then went for his bike. He was sure his brother was all right. In the same way Ice had found his way home, so would George. It was there, drawn for all to see.

He needed to go someplace where he could calm down, where he could think. He made his way to the old wooden water tower by the train station. Parking his bike, he stuffed his comics into the sleeves of his coat, tied it around his waist and climbed the rope ladder to the top.

Struggling, he heaved himself onto the platform that ran around the outside of the water cistern, then stood at the metal guardrail. The view was spectacular. The lights were dazzling and Robert marvelled at how big the city was. Although the weather had been unseasonably warm, the night air was cooling down rapidly. He took the comics out of his coat and put it on.

Sitting with his back against the wall of the cistern, he settled in to read, then realized it was too dark and he should have brought a flashlight. "What an idiot!"

"I'm not arguing with that, Wonder Weed."

Robert jumped, his heart in his throat. "Holy Hannah! Charlie, you scared me half to death!" He hastily stood up.

"Who else, besides me, would be wacky enough to be up here freezing their hiney off at nine o'clock on an October night?" She walked into the wan light of the rising moon. "Oh wait, I guess your hiney ain't exactly warm either."

"What are you doing up here?" Robert asked as his pulse slowed to normal.

"Bringing you a reading lamp for your dopey pulp fiction." She reached into her backpack and pulled out a flashlight, then switched it on. "Why aren't you snuggled in your jammies in your nice warm house reading those for a bedtime story?" She shined the beam on his comics.

"You wouldn't believe me if I told you." He slumped against the wood.

She came to sit beside him. "Good thing it's still so nice out. We could be squatting waist deep in snow. So, why are you up here?"

"My brother's plane was shot down over France and we found out tonight. A friend of my mum's who is with the RCAF came to tell us."

"Oh, Rob, I'm so, so sorry."

She sounded sincere, and when Robert saw her face, he knew she was genuinely upset. "Honestly, he's okay, Charlie. I know it. The problem is no one will believe me."

"You *know* it or you *hope* it? After all those terrible telegrams we've been delivering, I wouldn't blame you for pushing away from the truth."

"I *know* he's fine." He absently rubbed his amulet, feeling it warm against his skin.

"How?" She waited for an answer.

"If I told you, you'd think I was nuts."

"That ship has sailed, buddy boy. Try me anyway." She moved closer to him and pointed the flashlight at their feet.

Robert felt her body next to his. Maybe it was just the shared warmth, but surprisingly, he found he liked her being so close. "You sure?"

"Remember who you're talking to, Wonder Weed. This is Crazy Charlie Donnelly. I wrote the book on nuts. Ask any of your pals at school."

"Those idiots are not my friends, and definitely not what I call good judges of the real deal."

"I guess that makes me your best audience. So tell me how you know your brother is not dead."

Robert's head jerked up sharply at her bluntness. "Who said anything about dead?"

"The military doesn't make house calls unless it's something terminal."

"They don't know what's happened to him. Only I do." He took a deep breath. "You see, I have this connection, with the universe, and I get information through..." He hesitated, then plunged on, "Through my comic books. They tell me what's happening with my brothers, or they have since I found my meteorite."

Charlie puffed out a breath of air. "Whoa, cowboy, back it up. You mean the neck thing you always wear? It's a real meteorite? And you think it somehow plugs you into a weird cosmic telephone exchange that feeds you information?"

Robert winced. It did sound insane. "Actually, yes. And I get the messages through these three comic book heroes." He took the flashlight from her and shined the beam on the colourful covers. "Captain Ice; Sedna of the Sea; and the best hero in any universe – the Maple Leaf Kid." He then explained about finding the meteorite and how each of his comics had storylines that reflected exactly what was happening to his brothers. "...and their letters confirmed everything. Patrick, we're real close, he even saw the very same meteorite on the night I found it." He was caught up in the excitement now, and showed her Ice's story with the flyer being shot down over France. "I got this today and then I found out about George. If everything holds true, we should hear about the French resistance getting him to the coast soon."

Charlie sat silently beside him.

"So, what do you think? Am I in the Charlie Donnelly Crazy Club?" he asked.

"Oh, yeah, in fact, you're the president, pal." She elbowed him in the ribs.

"Anyway, I tried to tell my parents all this, but they won't believe me. I'm here to cool off so I don't make things worse." He turned to her, "Why is your butt up here?"

Charlie didn't answer him. Instead, she took the flashlight back and flipped the switch on and off, while pointing it up at her face, creating a bizarre strobe effect.

It was during one of those split seconds, as the light was shining on her, that Robert saw the vulnerability behind her tough-girl exterior.

"Hey, you don't have to tell me anything, except to mind my own business." He elbowed her this time.

"Let me put it this way, Wonder Weed: not all the war zones are overseas, and I hate being caught in the crossfire when the bottles start flying."

Robert knew there were families where drinking and fighting were normal, but he'd never dreamed she came from one of those. He felt she'd told him something in confidence. "That's rough, Charlie."

"I guess we both have worlds no one else understands. Now, let's see what's in those paper crystal balls of yours."

They read the comic books until the flashlight battery died and they both knew it was very late. Neither of them cared.

"Are you going to be okay, you know, going home tonight?" Robert asked as he held the ladder for Charlie to climb down.

"Oh, yeah. By now, both my parents will be passed-out drunk. I can sneak in my bedroom window like I was there enjoying the show all night long."

"About what I told you..." Robert was having second thoughts.

"What? I don't remember anything insane and certifiable you told me tonight. I spent a couple of hours reading comic books with a pal. End of story."

He grinned at her gratefully.

"Remember, if you were to receive a cosmic message, beamed in from outer space, I would expect to be told, Wonder Weed."

She waved as she walked toward her bike, which she'd stashed in some bushes near the ladder.

Robert felt a whole lot better as he slid through the darkened streets on his way home. When considering Crazy Charlie Donnelly, a lot of words came to mind, but until tonight, "friend" had never been one of them.

CHAPTER EIGHTEEN

SUKCES

THE WEEKEND TESTED ROBERT to his limits. Every minute, he expected Squadron Leader Aberdeen to show up, or the phone to ring with news of George being rescued by the French Resistance. His parents worried and Robert waited. Still, there was no news by Monday.

Charlie was loitering at the school doors when he arrived. "Well, Wonder Weed? Anything to report from your way-out connection?"

"Nothing so far. It will come through though, you can bet on it. Maybe tonight." He was sure the good news was on its way and wished it would hurry up. Sometimes the universe dragged its feet. He absently touched the talisman under his shirt. "You ready for another week of telegram tag?"

"Yup. I've got my uniform all spruced up and ready to go." She patted her backpack.

"Me too." He showed her his own shoulder carryall he'd borrowed from James' closet. "See you later, alligator."

AT WORK, THEY WERE met by four telegrams each.

"I tried to keep the addresses together so you can deliver them on one run." Mr. Crabtree said. He pushed the two stacks he'd arranged across the counter.

Robert and Charlie looked at each other as they reached for them and their boss read their faces: "Don't worry. You'll get paid for four deliveries. I'm trying to save you some time. If we have another week like last one, you'll be burnt out by Wednesday. Now go."

Smiling, Charlie and Robert left for their delivery runs. Robert's turned out to be businesses all within a few blocks, and Charlie's were in three neighbourhoods running in a straight line down Fourth Street.

Robert was back before Charlie and put the tea on for their break. When she didn't show after half an hour, he became concerned.

"Telegram!" Mr. Crabtree called from the counter and Robert went to get it.

"Do you know what happened to Donnelly?" his boss asked, slapping the delivery onto the counter.

"Maybe one of the people had bad news and Charlie stayed to help. Myself, I've been working on showing CPR Telegraphs as a real caring company." Robert hoped this made Charlie sound like a kind and thoughtful employee. Not as kind and thoughtful as him, of course.

"I know what was in those telegrams and there's no reason for her to dilly-dally. I hope I wasn't wrong in keeping a female on." He retreated to the back room and Robert left.

Robert checked the address and noticed it was quite near his own house in Pleasant Heights. He delivered the message in record time and was on his way back to the office when he spotted Charlie pushing her bike along the street. "Did your old wreck finally give up the ghost?"

"The stupid chain broke and I can't fix it. Worse, I don't have the money to buy a new one."

Robert wondered what she did with her pay. Maybe she blew it on sodas and burgers or movies.

"If Crabtree finds out I'm not reliable, he'll can me for sure. I need this job."

She sounded so upset, Robert felt sorry for her. He thought back a couple of weeks – how he would have laughed at her predicament then. What a difference a little time could make!

"I think I can help. Come on." He led her down a couple of streets and up an alley. They stopped in front of a familiar garage door.

"This is Glowinski's Repair Shop. Best fix-it shop in Calgary. Mr. G will have Big Betsy back to work in no time." Robert knocked on the side door of the garage and was rewarded when his neighbour answered.

"Robcio, what you doing here? Thought you work till seven?" It was then he noticed Charlie standing in the alley. "Surprise visitor?"

"Mr. G, this is Charlie...Charlene Donnelly, another telegram delivery...person. Her bike chain is broken and we're wondering if you could fix it."

"I make inspection." He nodded at Charlie. "Bring here, please, miss."

Charlie took the bike and the broken chain over to the repairman.

"Does it have to be replaced?" Her face was pained. "Is it going to be expensive?"

Mr. G took the bike and the chain and disappeared into the garage.

"Rob, you need to get back right away. It's not your problem and Crabtree will want someone's head on a platter."

"I live close to here. I'll tell him I wanted to check on my mum because she's so upset about George being shot down. He'll understand."

Charlie surveyed the tidy back fences and tall trees. "Wow, nice neighbourhood. How far from here do you live?"

Robert jerked his head at the house across the alley from the repair shop. "Not far. In fact, I think I will see if there's any news." He handed her his bike, then hustled into the house. Seconds later, he returned, unsmiling. "Nothing yet.

They waited until finally, Mr. G opened the wide swinging

door of the garage and wheeled the bike out, chain in place and sporting new skinnier tires. He gave it to Charlie.

"Chain fixed. Had master link. Also, old tires worn out. Going to be flat very soon. Big tires no good for delivery person. Takes much energy to push peddals around. Narrower make more sense. I rig it so wheels with better tires will work and put on."

Charlie admired the new tires and repaired chain. "This is the best!" Then she shook her head. "I'm sure I can't afford it. I'm sorry, but you'll have to put the old tires back on." She pushed the bike back at Mr. Glowinski.

Robert stepped forward. "Don't worry, Charlie. I did some work for Mr. Glowinski and he owes me money. What say we call it square – the money you owe me can go toward the repair bill, Mr. G? If there's any left over, you can give it to me later." He hoped the big man would figure out what he was trying to do.

"Ah, *tak, tak*. I remember now. Much money I owe you, Robcio. This much better way to do business – barter system, like old country."

"Great! Then it's all taken care of. I'll come and see you later and we can straighten out the details." As Charlie looked away, he mouthed a silent, "thank you" to his neighbour.

"I'll pay you back on Friday, Rob." Charlie said quickly. "And thank you again for fixing my bike so fast, Mr. Glowinski. Now, we'd better hightail it or old man Crabtree will have both our guts for garters." In the next second, Charlie was on her bike pedalling down the alley.

Robert started to join her, when Mr. Glowinski stopped him.

"Robcio, I told you girl problem change when you get older. I guess you older."

Robert thought the corner of Mr. G.'s mouth may have curved the tiniest bit as he went back into his garage.

The new skinnier tires made a big difference and Robert found himself working hard to keep up with Charlie. When they rolled back into work, Charlie marched up to the desk and, before Robert could spin his yarn, called Mr. Crabtree over to explain.

"We're late back because of me, boss. My bike broke down and when I saw Robert I asked if he could help. He knew someone so we took a few minutes and had it fixed. I thought it was better to have two rolling delivery people than leave you in the lurch."

Mr. Crabtree patiently listened to the story, then without a word, went to the desk and came back with two more telegrams for each of them. "These need delivering. I hope your freshly repaired bike is up to it, *Miss* Donnelly?"

"Yes, sir," Charlie mumbled as she took the letters.

"And you, Robert. I'd never have had you pegged for the white knight type." He slapped down Robert's telegrams. "Now go, the pair of you, before I put my ad back in the window."

WHEN ROBERT RETURNED home later, all the lights in his house were ablaze.

Going directly to the living room, he saw his parents sitting together on the couch, never a good sign. "Mum, Dad, what's happened?"

His mother rushed over to hug him. "Robert, Squadron Leader Aberdeen was here with the most wonderful news. George is alive! When he bailed out, he landed near the coast at Calais and a local fishing boat took him back to England. He's safe and well!"

Robert felt like he'd been vindicated. He'd been right. His comic books had been right. The whole darn universe had been right! "It's like I told you!" he said excitedly. "I knew it!"

"Not exactly," his father corrected. "Still, I'm not looking a gift horse in the mouth. I don't care how it happened; all I care about is that our boy is safe." He took his handkerchief out of his back pocket and swiped at his face.

"And on top of this wonderful news," his mother interrupted, "Letters came today from all your brothers, including George. Of course, he wrote before this whole thing happened so it will be strange to read. I put them on your bed, dear."

She was as close to babbling as Robert had ever heard. "This is the best day ever!" He thought of his fantastic superheroes and said a silent thank you.

They ate supper with happy hearts and Robert related the story of Crazy Charlie's bicycle trauma and how Mr. Glowinski had fixed everything up.

"Which reminds me, I guess I'd better go make things right with Mr. G. I owe him some money for the repairs."

"Why don't you go now? Then you can get to your letters before it's too late, dear." His mother's generosity was overwhelming, and like his dad, he wasn't going to look a gift horse in the mouth, especially the lead mare of this stable.

Robert left the table and was at the back door when he stopped. He quickly retrieved the kitchen garbage, then took the bag to the barrel in the alley before going to his neighbour's door and knocking.

When Mr. Glowinski answered, Robert tried to hurriedly explain. "Charlie really needs her job; it's super important to her, Mr. G. She was so upset when the old bike cratered – you wouldn't believe how someone gouged her on the price of that thing – so when the chain broke and you fixed it and the tires, I didn't want her to worry and that's why I said you owed me money and she didn't have to pay. I'm sorry about the white lie. I get paid on Friday and will bring you money for the work, I promise. Oh, and George is fine. He's safely back in England." He ran out of words and breath.

"Good news about brother. I glad to hear." Mr. Glowinski calmly folded the rag he was holding. "There is something we do back in Poland, I think good idea in new Canadian home."

Robert listened politely.

"When friend come to you for help, you help. No money needed. It is the right thing to do, so you do it. Only thing we need to decide is if we friends. What you think, Robcio?"

Robert thought about this and realized this was exactly what they were. "*Tak, tak*, we are friends," he agreed. "*Dziękuję*, Mr. G."

IN HIS ROOM, Robert stood before his brothers' pictures and saluted. "Welcome home, Georgie boy. What kept you?" He patted the top of the picture frame.

Picking up the newest comic book adventures from their stacks, he climbed onto his bed, arranged them beside him, and then tore open the first of his letters.

It was from George and related news about how they were flying further into French territory every mission. He hoped the enemy never caught on to what they were doing, because there would be a lot of guns to fly over on the way back. "You were right about the guns, George," Robert told his brother. He placed the letter on top of Ice's story of the French Resistance.

Next was beautiful Sedna with her pod of orcas and the supply ship. Skimming James' letter, he read about how his brother and the band of beach patrollers had watched a badly-damaged ship being towed into the harbour by two fishing trawlers. Almost exactly like Sedna's story.

Robert took his time decoding Patrick's letter. He liked to imagine every scene.

> *Buongiorno Roberto,*
>
> *Grazie for the home-grown care package, loved the Juicy Fruit gum and Sen Sen candy. Hey, what's with the Métis sash? I suspect our dear cousin Kathryn put you up to this. You know I don't go for the family history stuff, but it was fun to think of you squirming as Katy cornered you into sending it. We'll figure out what to do with it when I get home. Ha ha.*

Robert tapped the page with the pencil he'd used to decode the letter. There was a very good chance he'd end up with the sash. In fact, he'd put money on it.

> *We've been madly building Bailey bridges to cross what seems like the thousands of Italian rivers we are encountering.*

Great invention. They can even take the weight of a tank! The Krauts have a nasty habit of blowing the existing bridges as they retreat, and the ones we find intact need a thorough going-over by the sappers. I'm liking the food (Mum will have to make gnocchi for me) and have discovered a taste for Chianti.

The rest of the letter was boring. Patrick rambled on about several Italian ladies he'd also "discovered" as the Canadians marched from town to town. This avid interest in the women, along with the Chianti comment, was new for Patrick. Robert wondered what changes he would see in all his brothers when they came home.

Finishing the letter, Robert held *The Maple Leaf Kid* up and peered at the cover closely. He concentrated and squeezed his pendant tightly. There, in the lower right corner, the soldier in front of the first tank...was that Patrick? Robert leaned in, focusing. He felt like he could step into the picture, reach out and touch his brother. It was so real. Tentatively, he extended his fingertips and –

"Robert, I expect those letters when you're done with them!" His mother's voice floated up to him from somewhere below.

THE ENEMY WAS RIGHT ON HIS TAIL! OUR HERO HAD NO WHERE TO HIDE AND HIS BRIGHTLY COLOURED LITTLE FIGHTER WAS HARD TO MISS. HE HIT THE OIL SWITCH, FLOODING HIS ENGINE, WHICH COUGHED OUT A CLOUD OF GRIMY SMOKE; OUR HERO SPED AWAY AS HIS ENEMY WAS ENVELOPED IN THE BLINDING BLACKNESS.

Satisfied all his universes were in order, Robert replaced the comics in their correct piles with the decoded versions of the letters hidden inside, then returned the originals to their envelopes for his mother to enjoy. With a little luck, she wouldn't ask him about the secret code copies.

CHAPTER NINETEEN

GHOSTS OF GREASE PAST

NOVEMBER WAS UNUSUAL for a lot of reasons. Temperatures were still up and snowfall was down, both of which Robert was very grateful for. Delivering telegrams on snowy, icy streets wasn't his idea of a good time, though complaining was out of the question when he thought of Charlie. She still peddaled all the way from Bowness to school, then delivered until seven and, finally, faced the long trek back to her house on the west side of the city. All he had to do was shoot across the river to his welcoming home, fifteen minutes away.

"I think our pay should be higher in the winter." Charlie sat sipping hot tea at the staff table, still in her toque and scarf, boots firmly stuck on her feet. "We could negotiate with our kind boss."

Robert blew on his hot tea. "Are we talking union here?" His voice an imitation of a tough guy from the movies. "Strike, maybe?"

Since George's adventures in France, Robert and Charlie's truce had deepened. As it turned out, she wasn't the evil Satan-incarnate he'd originally thought. She was only a girl.

"*Strike* is a hard word…" she said thoughtfully. "And an expensive one. Think of all those three-centers you'd miss out on while you're walking the picket line."

"Telegram!" Mr. Crabtree's booming call interrupted their discussion.

"That's me!" Charlie jumped up, grabbing her coat and mittens.

"Yeah, yeah. Later." Robert went back to reading a copy of the Kid he'd brought. Studying the page, he saw himself standing shoulder to shoulder with his hero, working with him to solve whatever problem threatened. He liked the way the artist put a red maple leaf on the pocket of the kid's white shirt, which was always buttoned all the way to the top. It made him seem kind of goofy, which had worked in the Kid's favour many times when an enemy had underestimated his brilliant mind.

The other two heroes waited their turn. Lately, he found if he didn't read all three every day, he got sort of...antsy. He knew the link with his brothers and their guardians depended on his vigilance, and so he read and reread the comics, noticing details he'd missed before: expressions on characters' faces, numbers on ships, different flora and fauna to help him pinpoint the country the story took place in. Robert understood it was his job to commit all these details to memory to ensure they were kept real. After all, what if he didn't see the olive trees in the scene? Then maybe the Kid wouldn't concentrate on Italy as the specific country to help, and he had to keep the Kid in Italy with Patrick.

His meteorite hummed. The vivid cover illustration was like a tiny slice of a special world and he was watching this other world through the portal of his comic book. He stroked the bright colours, so beautiful, and the detail – incredible. Whoever created this masterpiece was a magician.

Robert knew the story practically word for word. He could speak the part of the Maple Leaf Kid out loud and knew all of the actions drawn in the panels. Without much effort at all, he could have been the Kid. He flipped his hair, now thankfully grown back, off his forehead, the same way the Kid did.

A tap on his shoulder made him flinch. It was Mr. Crabtree with a telegram.

"Tarnation, Tourond, didn't you hear me hollering?"

Robert guiltily jumped to his feet, stashing the Kid in his

knapsack. "Gosh, no sir, Mr. Crabtree. Sorry, sir."

Grabbing the telegram, he put on his winter gear and left. It was only after he was outside that he read the name. It was his teacher, Miss Alice Pettigrew.

Thinking of all those ghastly telegrams, Robert really didn't want to deliver a message he knew would devastate his teacher and change her life forever. She was a little strange, maybe a whole bushel basket full of strange, and yet he liked her and had learned more from her than any other teacher. She had a way of explaining things so you not only understood them, you also wanted to find out more.

The north wind was unusually bitter and stung his face as he made his way through the dark, icy streets. He tried to think of what he would say, or how he'd be able to help when his teacher read the terrible news he was carrying. He knew how the Angel of Death must feel.

Miss Pettigrew lived in a small apartment building and, according to the address, she was in number six, which turned out to be the basement suite at the back. Steeling himself against what was coming, Robert knocked.

His teacher opened the door with a cigarette in one side of her mouth. Her hair was tangled in big curlers that resembled soup cans, and she had green goop slathered all over her face.

"Howdy, Robert!" Her cheerful reaction quickly changed and Robert figured she must be imagining how she looked to a student. "My goodness, you've caught me at kind of an awkward moment." She touched her face and her fingers came away green.

"Telegram for Miss Alice Pettigrew." He tried to sound very professional and solemn. He'd seen how folks dissolved when they read these things and wanted to give the situation the gravity it deserved.

Pencil-drawn eyebrows furrowed in confusion. Then he held up the envelope and comprehension flooded Miss Pettigrew's face as she recognized his uniform. "You'd better come in." Stepping back, she swung the door wide.

Robert walked into the warm apartment, then held out his

delivery book for her to sign. He'd discovered that once folks had their telegram, everything else was forgotten – like signing his book – and he'd have to explain to Mr. Crabtree why he had no proof of delivery.

She ripped open the telegram and Robert watched her closely.

Next, she sat down hard on the chair by the door. "I don't believe it!"

He waited for the inevitable.

"This is, is..." She took the cigarette she'd been puffing on out of her mouth and blew a smoke ring into the air.

Robert was ready to get a neighbour.

"*Fabulous!*" she squealed in a very undevastated way.

This was not what he'd expected. Either the news wasn't a death notice, or his teacher was wackier than he'd thought.

She jumped up and started dancing. "Who's going to be spotlighted?" she asked the apartment. "I'm going to be spotlighted!" she answered herself, giving her hip a bump to the left.

"I guess it's good news then."

"*Good?* It's *great!*" She continued to shimmy around her apartment. "Do you read comics, Robert?"

This was another unexpected turn. "As a matter of fact, I do."

"I do, too. It's my guilty secret." She put one finger to her lips and then sashayed over to a table beside her sofa and picked up a comic book.

Robert's mouth fell open in surprise. It was *The Maple Leaf Kid*, September edition.

His teacher went on, "In the back of the comic is a contest where you write in about doing something big for the war effort and if you're chosen, you get spotlighted nationally."

He knew about this in spades. It still stung a little when he thought of losing to Charlie.

She took a drag on her cigarette, then went on. "So, I wrote to the comic book people about the splendid success of the Great Grease Roundup and how, because of the contest, we collected more fat than any school in the entire district, in fact, our school collected more fat than any school in Alberta! We massacred those suckers. I suggested if every school in Canada had a similar contest, it would make a real impact on the war effort." She waved the telegram at him. "The comic book folks agreed! They are going to spotlight yours truly in the December issue and my Great Grease Roundup so other kids can take the idea to their schools. Imagine what a difference it will make if each student works as hard as you and Charlene! In fact, I'll be sure to mention your names in the article." She paused a heartbeat. "Plus, I will be one important gal at the next Teachers' Development Day."

Robert's mouth dropped open. This was salt in the wound! This was vinegar poured into an open cut! This was...he stopped and thought about it. Actually, this was incredible! Instead of the one-issue spotlight his story would have made if he'd won, as a teacher, Miss Pettigrew's spotlight would be taken more seriously and her idea could snowball into the greatest war effort since, well, since they'd needed a war effort.

He couldn't help it. He started to laugh. He'd come here thinking he was bringing the worst news ever, instead he was going back knowing he and Charlie had actually done something important. They may have started a movement that would show kids how each and every one of them could be real heroes. He could hardly wait to tell his old arch enemy.

THE NEXT DAY, he and Charlie were sitting at the break table as he related what had happened at Miss Pettigrew's. He drew the story out, describing every detail of his encounter with their eccentric teacher, from her cigarette smoke ring and green face goop, to the celebratory drink of sweet sherry she poured herself as she saw him to the door. It had been the most interesting telegram delivery he'd ever had.

"So you see, Charlie, our over-the-top efforts in the fat contest are going to have a huge effect. Our little competition may be the start of something big." He tipped his head at her. "It takes the bite out of me losing and you winning by one lousy pound."

Charlie's face went crimson. "Ah, Robert...about that," she stumbled over her words. "You see..."

Robert waited.

"About the contest..." she rasped. Then she coughed to clear her throat, as if her words were choking her.

"Yeah, I know. You won, I lost; it was close and I really wanted those dumb stamps. We both pulled out all the stops, Charlie. That's not the point now. Back then, you and I, well..." He was embarrassed to be talking so personally, practically baring his soul to her. "We weren't exactly pals. You could say we were like..." He paused and remembered Miss Pettigrew's class on Canadian history. "...like Wolfe and Montcalm. I want you to know it's all changed now." When they were competing, he wouldn't have blinked if the earth had opened up and sucked her down whole. He didn't feel the same way anymore, not by a long shot. He had to admit it: she was his best friend.

Charlie hesitated, an anxious expression on her face, and Robert wondered what was up. "I've never seen you run out of words before," he laughed. "And you're so serious. Come on, what is it, Donnelly!"

She took a deep breath, then everything came pouring out in a torrent, "I cheated to win the stupid contest. I knew you had me with your Hail Mary delivery Friday morning and I snuck back later and added a little insurance to my vat o' fat. I took some out of your tub and transferred it to mine, enough to make sure I won."

Robert was stunned. "You cheated in the contest? You rigged it?"

Charlie was the picture of guilt as she hurried on. "I had to. You don't understand. I needed those stamps. Okay, technically I needed the money I'd get for them. I had to win."

His mind was spinning. "And you think I didn't need the money?"

"You've got it so easy with your white picket fence-house and two nice parents. It wasn't as important for you."

Robert thought of his comic book link to his brothers and how he needed it to keep them safe. She could have cost him his brothers. Rage boiled up, white hot. "You have no idea how important winning was to me. You had no right! You stole that money from me!"

"You don't get it." She tried to defend what she'd done. "I had to win!"

He stood so quickly, his chair toppled over backward. "I don't want to hear your excuses."

Reaching for his arm, Charlie tried to stop him. "I'm really sorry, Rob. You have to believe me."

He jerked his arm out of her grasp. "Stay away from me. *Just stay the hell away!*"

He stalked to the front counter to wait for the next delivery.

CHAPTER TWENTY

NEVER FORGOTTEN, NEVER FORGIVEN

ROBERT COULDN'T BRING himself to forgive Charlie for her betrayal. She had no idea how close to disaster losing the fat contest had put him. If he hadn't been able to get those comic books, there was no telling what would have happened to his brothers. Her confession changed things. He did his job without speaking to his enemy or helping her in any way. She was a liar, a cheater and a thief. He was done with her.

"I don't know who peed in whose cornflakes, but you two had better straighten things out pronto," Mr. Crabtree ordered one afternoon.

"Some things can't be straightened out." Robert took the telegram from his boss and slammed out the door.

For him, it was now all about the work. He didn't talk to Charlie, or sit with her, or listen when she tried to explain her betrayal. He imagined the disasters that might have befallen his brothers if he hadn't been able to buy the comics. It made him seethe every time he thought about it, and he thought about it all the time.

Instead, Robert was so focused on his job, his delivery times sped up as he became more familiar with the city. Not enough to beat the record-setting Crazy Charlie Donnelly, but he was definitely narrowing the gap.

Returning from his last delivery late one evening, Robert saw Charlie struggling to drag her bike out of a slushy puddle at the side of the road. She must have slipped on the icy corner. It was snowing and the air had a bitter bite to it. He didn't even slow down as he barrelled past. He didn't care.

DESPITE CHARLIE DONNELLY's betrayal, Robert had a spring in his step when he walked into Mr. Kreller's drugstore Friday evening. He had money in his pocket and, as his meteorite had been fizzing all day, he knew something good was about to happen.

"You are one lucky young man, Robert. The two lads came in yesterday and the lady arrived today. Should I wrap all three?"

Robert shivered, as much from anticipation as from the chilly ride there. His heroes were over a week late and he'd been worried something apocalyptic had happened in the world of Canadian comic books.

"You bet, Mr. Kreller. November will go out with a roar." All three of his heroes and the weekend to savour them. Yowser! He was going to hunker down and seriously study his magical books. Robert knew that each time he read them, he would see more and have a better understanding of what was really in the story. It was as if layers were laid down like sediment and the only way to fully understand the messages hidden there was to keep reading the comics over and over again.

The ride home through the darkened streets was one of the fastest he'd ever done. He could hardly wait.

He'd received letters from his brothers this week and wanted to see how his superheroes dealt with the same problems his brothers had encountered.

Turning down his mother's offer of a hot meal, he grabbed a sandwich and went straight to his room. After greeting his brothers' pictures, he hopped on his bed and withdrew the precious tomes. His attention ricocheted from one vividly drawn cover to another. They were spectacular, and so well done he could have sworn he saw the waves moving beneath Sedna's feet and the propellers whirling on Ice's plane.

The cover of the Kid's comic was special, that was obvious. He was with the Canadian troops in a combat situation. Everyone crowded around him as he likely explained some brilliant plan to thwart the enemy. Robert would save the Kid for last so he could take his time.

Again, the storylines and his brothers' letters coincided so closely, Robert was amazed.

James and Sedna had spent days executing a devious way to stop the enemy from coming into the harbours they were protecting. James had commandeered three fishing boats to tow a large section of a wrecked pier into the mouth of the harbour. It was safe for fishing boats who knew the shallow channel, but not for deep-water submarines. Sedna had used her sea creatures to push a large iceberg into place to stop a fleet attacking Canadian merchant ships in the north Atlantic, and when the enemy had changed course to avoid the floating mountain of ice, they had run aground on a submerged reef. Almost exactly the same, pretty much.

George and Ice were back flying and they'd both blown up enemy installations, damaging supply lines in a big way. This was George's job and he did it well.

"In fact, Ice," Robert said, "George could probably teach you a thing or two about taking out bridges." He thought he saw the cartoon fighter pilot grin wryly in agreement.

He placed both these comics and the letters back with the appropriate brother then settled in for the Maple Leaf Kid's adventure.

The Kid was in Italy delivering a secret weapon he'd invented. The machine broadcast a unique signal that knocked out all enemy communications, rendering them blind and helpless. Plus, as an added bonus, the reflection would tell the allies where the German troops were hiding. Our boys could pick off truck convoys, tanks, troops and even battleships shrouded in fog as they waited to attack.

It was ingenious and only the Kid knew how to operate the complicated piece of machinery. At the big climax, a German spy stole the machine right before a crucial battle, then tried to kidnap the Kid so the Nazis could use the machine against the Allies. As the spy closed in, the Kid set the dial to the special frequency and turned on the machine, knowing the high-pitched noise would knock out whoever heard it. Our savvy hero, safely wearing good-old Canadian ear muffs, was immune to the noise blast. With the spy out cold, the Kid escaped and was able to get the wondrous machine back to the Allies, ensuring the good guys won the day.

Robert felt drawn into the story. The walls of his room wavered, shimmering with an incandescent light, then disappeared. He was there, alongside the Maple Leaf Kid as he tuned his machine to do maximum signal interruption. Robert could taste the dust in the dry air, feel the hot Mediterranean sun on his face and smell the foul breath of the despicable spy. The noise of the guns was deafening and Robert winced as the shock waves from the explosions hit his body.

With a start, he peered around at his familiar bedroom. The blurred walls wavered; then came into focus again. He'd never experienced a comic book adventure quite like this before. It was so real!

He had an odd sensation and realized that he was clutching his pendant. When had he done that? He didn't remember but it must have been some time ago. His fingers were stiff and sore and there was a mark as red as a burn in the centre of his palm.

THE DAYS MARCHED BY and soon it was December. The temperature dropped and Robert bundled up as much as he could while still allowing movement to pedal. Mr. Crabtree gave them leather gaiters to strap to their lower legs to help with the snow and cold. Robert wondered how Charlie could stand it; she never seemed to wear as many clothes as he did. He pushed down his sympathy, though, and told himself it was a good thing: it kept the playing field level. He'd be cornered with a bayonet sooner than admit he missed the warmth of their friendly banter.

One night after supper, Robert took the garbage out before his mother could pester him and noticed the light was on in Mr. G's workshop. Robert had been too busy to see his friend in a while, and after all the miles he'd put on his wheeled wonder this last week, his chain could really use some oil. It was a good time to drop by. He walked over and let himself in the side door to the shop.

"Hey Mr. G, I was wondering if you had any chain lube? I'm really running up the miles and..."

Time stopped as Robert's mind tried to make sense of what he saw.

Mr. Glowinski stood illuminated by the pale glow of the yellow overhead light. His face was haggard, gray and drawn, his tortured eyes red-rimmed.

In his hand was a pistol.

The barrel rested against his temple.

CHAPTER TWENTY-ONE

MEN AND MONSTERS

FROZEN, ROBERT DIDN'T KNOW what to do. He was scared even to breathe.

"Mr. G," he finally whispered, "has something happened?" It was a stupid thing to ask, as obviously something had happened to drive him to this.

His neighbour didn't seem to hear him.

Robert wanted to run, to get someone, but was terrified of what Mr. Glowinski would do if he left. Still, the urge to escape was almost overpowering. Then he thought of all the help and the friendship this quiet man had given him.

The pendant around Robert's neck warmed, the temperature climbing, heat increasing. The power of the amulet pushed him forward. He took a hesitant step further into the garage. "What can I do? Can I get you something? A cup of tea maybe?" He could have kicked himself for that one, too. Again, a ridiculous thing to say, but tea had always been his fallback in dire situations and this was the direst. He was trying to be calm, afraid of startling his neighbour and perhaps causing his finger to jerk.

Mr. Glowinski blinked, then shook himself, as if awakening from a long ago memory, a long ago nightmare. He lowered the pistol and placed it on the workbench as casually as if it were merely another tool, a wrench or a screwdriver.

The big man ran his rough palm down his face, trying to scrape away some unbearable pain. "No, no, Robcio, nothing can be done."

Robert watched him collapse heavily onto a wooden stool, the weight of an unseen world crushing him. "This anniversary of very bad thing that happened. Every night I dream of this thing."

"Something back in Poland?" Robert asked quietly.

"*Tak, tak.*" Mr. G shuddered. "You don't need to know this sadness. It eat your soul, make you want to end pain."

Robert's necklace felt hot against his skin again and he found himself taking another step closer. "Mr. G, my nan always said, 'A burden shared is a burden halved.' Especially if the trouble is shared with a friend."

Mr. Glowinski's tragic eyes stared into some distant past, and then he nodded in silent agreement. "Four years ago today, Nazis marched into our village in *Polska*, what you call Poland. They rounded up men for slave labour, then herded all women and children into town square. My Marta and our babies, Jacob, four; and two-year-old Anya, all together. They made men watch as they..." His breath froze in his chest, and then he exhaled. "As they drove over our families with tanks."

Robert was struck speechless. Had he heard right? Had this quiet, kind man been forced to watch as his loved ones were brutally murdered in front of him?

He tried to recreate this horror in his mind, drawing the gruesome images as they would have been in the most violent of his comic books and still he couldn't comprehend it. It was unthinkable. He couldn't imagine seeing something so horrible and losing everyone he loved, and then having to live with the memory every day.

"Mr. G, I...I..." he stuttered. "I don't know what to say. Your whole family is gone?"

The broken man nodded, then gulped, trying to loosen his tongue. "I escape from guards, not caring if they shoot me, I have nothing to live for. Somehow, I make it to woods and then border. Farmer took me to refugee camp. I tell them I am electrical engineer and they send me to Canada. I ended up here."

He was hoarse when he spoke. "I tell you something, Robcio. When this happen, I would give anything, do anything, to change bad thing. I change reality, even, to save loved ones. My Marta would have liked Canada. It good country." Here he nodded at Robert. "Good people."

Robert had an inspiration. He quickly removed his pendant and held it out to Mr. Glowinski. "I think you should have this. It will make you feel, like...like you're part of something bigger, the universe, like we're all connected somehow. Maybe it will bring you closer to your family. Maybe they live among the stars now."

He could see Mr. G was about to refuse his gesture of goodwill, then the big man reached out and took the small meteorite.

The second the amulet left his fingertips, Robert felt bereft. He told himself he was like the Maple Leaf Kid, doing something for the greater good. "It's special, Mr. G, it has powers."

"I know this very important to you, Robcio, maybe most important thing for now. *Dziękuję, mój przyjacielu.*" He put his calloused hand on Robert's shoulder. "Thank you, my friend. I feel very good when I know you have it. You appreciate it." He gave the talisman back.

"Honest, Mr. G, it would make me feel so much better, like I've done something to help you." Robert searched for the words to make him understand. "Remember how you listened to my rant when I was having trouble with Crazy Charlie? Your listening helped me."

"Your friend with broken bike?"

"Yes, and we're back to being worst enemies again, by the way."

The shadow of something, which may have been a weak smile, passed across the weary man's face. "She hard worker. Maybe you two get along again someday."

Robert didn't bother to argue. Mr. G's weary voice told Robert the man had no heart left to fight about anything.

"I tell you what we do, Robcio. When I make your medallion, two pieces broke off. They still sit over there. I couldn't throw them out. I will make into same you have. I keep one and think about stars. You right. That will make me feel better, to see my Marta and my babies up there. They shine down on me."

"*Tak, tak*, Mr. G," Robert agreed. He squeezed his own star and wished peace for his friend and, perhaps, a dreamless night's sleep.

CHAPTER TWENTY-TWO

_____

STORM CLOUDS

DECEMBER WAS PASSING fast as Robert waited for the new adventures to show up. The Christmas issues were always a little more exciting than the rest; he guessed it was to wind up the year on a high note. It didn't help that Mr. Kreller said he'd been so busy, he hadn't put the December comic book order in with his supplier yet and they'd be late. Whatever the reason, Robert could hardly wait.

His mother had been wild about confiscating his wages lately, telling him he had to save more as she knew he wanted to buy another savings certificate before Christmas, which meant *she* wanted to buy another savings certificate before Christmas. At the rate she was making him save, he'd be the richest kid in Calgary, if not Canada, by the time the war was over. He stashed away enough to buy his Christmas comics when they came in, but did it in such a way that he didn't have to actually lie to his mum about his wages.

The week preceding Christmas, they were busier than ever, good for the pay cheque, but fighting the cold and holiday shopping traffic was exhausting.

"Telegram!"

Robert was oblivious to the call. He was busy helping Ice refuel his fighter plane before the Nazis storm troopers arrived.

Avgas was extremely flammable and it was always safer with two people.

"Rob, you're up," Charlie whispered.

Still he didn't respond.

"*Wonder Weed!*" She kicked him under the table. "Move it!" Robert jerked his head from the page. "What?" he snarled.

"Old man Crabtree called you. Delivery – unless you want me to take it?" Her voice was flint edged.

"You wish." He closed his comic and went to the desk.

"It's going to Mewata Armouries and fast. This one's a premium payer." The cigar in his boss's mouth danced when he spoke.

"I need it." Robert picked up the telegram.

The delivery took him the rest of his shift, but it was worth it. Although not the two-fifty he'd have received for a Bowness run, the twenty-five cents from the Mewata telegram would add nicely to his tally. It was only Wednesday and he was already way ahead of Crazy Charlie. There was no way she would out carn him this week.

On the way home, black storm clouds rolled in with frightening speed and the weather took a nasty turn. The needle-like sleet stung Robert's cheeks and made him wish he had flying goggles like Ice. They'd stop the millions of tiny knives slicing relentlessly at him.

As he pedalled through the darkness, he felt especially tired and chalked it up to the long trip to Mewata. He plowed on feeling worse every minute, and by the time he made it home, he felt really lousy. He stopped by Mr. Glowinski's to say hi, still worried things might again get desperate for his brave neighbour.

"Hey, Mr. G. How's tricks?" He tried to keep his tone light, which took a real effort now that he knew the tragic background of his friend.

"I better, thanks be to God and you, Robcio. Good you come. See this." His neighbour walked to the workbench and held up a pendant on a chain.

It was a smaller version of Robert's own, without the ornate metalwork. "I wait to show you. Now, I put on." With a grand gesture, he fastened the amulet around his neck. "I keep family close to my heart." He patted his broad chest.

Robert beamed at his friend. "This is very, very..." He scoured his mind for exactly the right word to fit this auspicious occasion. "This is very *dobre*. That means *good*, right?"

"That mean *good*, Robcio."

His neighbour smiled back and Robert understood it was genuine; this was a smile you could have faith in. A rush of heat from his own talisman let him know the universe had heard his message and, as the meteorite hummed in agreement, he knew Mr. G was going to have much better dreams from now on.

The happiness buoyed him up as he went into his own house but it didn't last, and as the evening wore on, he felt sick again. Not about his neighbour, he knew things would work out there. It was all physical. Chills, nausea and a wicked tiredness overcame him.

"Robert, are you all right?" his ever vigilant mother probed as they ate their late supper.

"A little tired. I'll be fine." He figured a good night's sleep was all he needed.

It didn't turn out that way. Thursday morning, Robert woke with a spiking fever and felt achy all over.

His mother couldn't be fooled this time. "No school for you, young man, or work either. You should phone your boss and let him know. I'll contact the school."

OUR HERO VALIENTLY TRIED TO ENGAGE THE ENEMY. SADLY, THERE WAS NO FIGHT LEFT IN HIM AND THEY BOTH KNEW IT. SWOOPING AWAY, THE ENEMY PLANE FLEW OFF ON ITS DEADLY MISSION WHILE HE LIMPED BACK TO THE HANGAR.

Robert called Mr. Crabtree and explained he was sick and couldn't come in for his shift.

"Sorry to hear you're under the weather. I must say, this is bad timing. We've got a slew of military telegrams to deliver and you know those are top priority, no excuses for being late with them. It's a bad one this time, Robert," he added confidentially. "There'll be a lot of grief in Calgary tonight. I'd help, except my dang key never stops chirping and I can't abandon it."

"I hate to let you down, Mr. Crabtree. I'll get some rest and I'm sure I'll be better by tomorrow. I'll be in right after school." As he hung up, Robert hoped it didn't sound like a hunk of baloney. He went back to bed, his head aching.

He slept between visits from his mother, who checked on him constantly and always managed to time it to the exact minute he was dozing off. He was as weak as a newborn babe, but found if he didn't move around he felt better. Lying in bed also allowed him to concentrate on his comic books and he pulled old issues out of the back of his closet to revisit long ago adventures.

Rest and his mother's constant stream of strong tea, eventually did its work and by late afternoon he was on the mend. He didn't want to miss any more shifts. He also didn't want Crazy Charlie to get any ideas about taking over all the deliveries and squeezing him out of a job. Retrieving a stack of comics from under his bed, Robert settled in for another reading session.

Without warning, his mother popped into his room, as cheery as one of Santa's elves.

"How are you feeling, sweetheart? Did the medicine help?" she asked, referring to the latest round of tea and dry toast. Bustling over, she placed her "mother hand" on his forehead. "Still 100 degrees. I was going to go to my Knit for Victory Club meeting. Instead, I think I should put you in a tepid bath and try to cool you down."

Robert's hope for a long uninterrupted session with his comics sank like a torpedoed frigate. Then his mother's reference to her knitting club gave him an idea.

"Mum, you can't possibly think of ditching the Knit for Victory Club. Think of all our boys over there waiting for their Christmas parcels and the nice warm socks you're making." His mother blinked rapidly as she considered this and Robert grew a tiny bit hopeful.

"I am so careful to use the Kitchener toe so they'll be comfy in those dreadful army boots they make our young men wear. I know if I'm not there, Mavis Blanchard won't take the time to do it right. It's tricky to knit you know."

"Oh, yes, Mum. If you aren't there to supervise, there's no telling what blister-busting stitch Mavis would use." He let this stew a minute, then added, "And blisters can lead to blood poisoning then, eventually, to gangrene. And you know what comes next – *the surgeon's bone saw!*"

"Don't be so melodramatic, Robert. Still, do you think you could wait while I go to my meeting? I won't be long as your dad will want his supper when he gets home and I promise you'll have an extra-long bath later."

Robert took his chance: "I insist you go, Mother. This is for my brothers, for *all* our boys, fighting so valiantly against *that Hitler!*"

She hurried out of his room as Robert flopped back on his bed and relaxed. Then he propped up his pillows, snagged his copy of *The Maple Leaf Kid* from under the quilt and settled in for a well-earned quest with his hero.

A dozen comic books later, Robert decided he needed a fresh supply of reading material and knew exactly where to get it: his secret milk-crate stash in the garage. Throwing back the covers, he grabbed his robe, stuck his feet in his slippers and went in search of more adventures.

After selecting a half-dozen favourite old epics, he was on his way back to bed when, as he passed through the living room, he happened to glance out the window and see Crazy Charlie turning onto his street.

She must be checking up on him to see if he really was sick, then, if she found him goldbricking, she could tattle to old man Crabtree.

Robert watched her lean her old cruiser against the front fence and open the gate. She was a piece of work and brazen, too, coming right to his door. And to think, at one time, he had liked her.

He decided a pre-emptive strike was best and opened the front door before she could reach the step. "No need to spy on me, Charlie. I really am sick, so you can report that news flash back to Crabtree!"

He stopped when he saw her face. She had tears in her eyes. Then he saw what she was holding.

CHAPTER TWENTY-THREE

DON'T SHOOT THE MESSENGER

IT TOOK ROBERT A SECOND to realize what he was seeing. Crazy Charlie wasn't here to check up on him. She was working. She had a delivery. She had a telegram and she was coming up his walk.

Heat built in his pendant, hotter and hotter. He felt the strange buzzing against his chest that came from the small interstellar rock when something was going to happen, something big.

What was it Mr. Crabtree had said? "It's a bad one this time" and "There'll be a lot of grief in Calgary tonight."

When George had been shot down, the air force had sent Squadron Leader Aberdeen to notify them. Since he wasn't here, it meant the telegram was about James or Patrick.

Robert shook his head. No. No telegrams for him about any of his brothers. Period. Final. Not going to happen. "You're not delivering anything here, Charlie."

She kept coming.

"It's a mistake. Crabtree must have written my address by mistake."

Charlie continued toward him.

He felt a drop of sweat run down his back. "I said it's not for here! Now, turn around and go tell the boss he screwed up the address!"

Charlie raised her arm, the telegram blazing in the evening light like a spectral message from beyond. "There's no mistake. It's for your family."

"I said it's not for us! Now, take off, Donnelly! Get back on that hunk of junk and leave!" He was yelling and his face felt hot.

She reluctantly climbed the porch steps. "I'm so sorry, Rob."

Robert shook his head. "Maybe one of them has been wounded and is on his way home. Yes, of course, one of my brothers is coming home for Christmas." He knew he was raving now. He could feel his heart racing wildly, adrenalin pumping.

Charlie reached out for him, but Robert shoved her back down the steps. "Get away! You're not my friend! I said one of my brothers will be home for Christmas. That's what's in your lousy telegram." Was this what it was like for all those people he'd delivered to? Had they felt like caged animals with no way out?

She climbed the steps again and planted herself firmly at the top in front of him. "What happened between us before, it's ancient history, Rob. What I have here," she held out the telegram again, "like it or not, this is the future and I'm not going to let you face it alone." Charlie spoke softly, like she didn't want to spook him as she tried to gently push him back toward the doorway.

"There's nothing wrong. This will be okay. Wait and see," Robert said, but he didn't budge.

"I know, Rob. Let's go inside where it's warm. I'm freezing out here."

Her attempt at being reassuring wasn't very convincing.

Too tired to fight, Robert allowed himself to be led back into the house. Charlie sat with him on the couch. He noticed there was snow on her lashes, making them glitter like they were dusted by diamonds.

He reached for the telegram and she pulled it away. "I have to give it to an adult. Are your folks home?"

"It's ridiculous that we're old enough to deliver those things but not old enough to receive them!" He had never thought the age rule would apply to him. "I think it stinks. We shouldn't be riding all over town, giving those out like so many underage

Grim Reapers." He was angry now. It was all so stupid.

Charlie sat and took it all: the yelling, the brutal words, everything.

There was a noise in the hall as Robert's mother bustled in the front door. They heard the sound of her taking off her boots and hanging up her coat.

"Robert!" She called up the stairs. "I'm home, dear! I'll pop the kettle on and make you a nice cup of tea."

She walked into the living room and stopped when she saw Charlie, in her grey CPR Telegraphs uniform, sitting beside Robert on the couch. "Oh, hello. I'm Helen Tourond, Robert's mother. You must be Charlie, his friend from work. Are you here to check up on our patient?" She asked brightly.

Charlie stood and faced Robert's mother. She tugged her coat down and cleared her throat.

"Actually, Mrs. Tourond, I'm here to deliver this telegram." She held the envelope out and Robert's mother staggered back a step.

"Is this a joke? If so, it's in very poor taste, young lady."

"It's no joke, Mrs. Tourond." Charlie stepped forward. "I'm so sorry to bring you this."

Still seeming not to understand, the shocked woman turned to her son. "Is this a mistake, Robert?"

Robert moved to stand beside Charlie. "No, Mum. There's no mistake. She's here on business."

Charlie turned to him. "And because I'm Rob's friend."

A noise from the kitchen signalled Robert's father had arrived.

"William, come here please!" Helen Tourond waited for her husband to come to the living room. "This is Charlie from Robert's work. She says she has a telegram for us." A message of understanding flowed between them.

"Nice to meet you, Charlie." Robert's dad solemnly accepted the telegram.

His parents sat together on the couch and opened the letter. Robert watched as his mother's face went through exactly the same sequence as every other person he'd delivered these to. He didn't need to be told what the telegram said.

"Oh, my God." His mother's hand went to her mouth as though to stifle a scream.

His father coughed to clear his throat. "They say Patrick is missing in action."

The words hit Robert like a fist.

His father went on with the details. "They were fighting outside a small town called Ortona in Italy. His patrol was sent to capture a German soldier for intelligence. The soldier threw a grenade, wounding some of Patrick's men, and Pat ordered his patrol to retreat to safety. Somehow, he became separated from them and never returned. More information will be forwarded as it becomes available."

His voice conveyed the bleakness they all felt. Robert's mother slumped into her husband's arms.

Charlie touched Robert to get his attention. "Maybe we should give your parents a moment alone. Let's take a walk."

Numbly, Robert followed Charlie upstairs. She found his room and made him sit on the bed, then wrapped a blanket around his shoulders.

"I know you're hurting, Rob. I wish I could help." She took in the room, her gaze lingering on his dresser with the stacks of comic books and pictures of his brothers.

Robert had added a candle for good measure. He thought the overall effect was perfect.

"Which one's Patrick?" Charlie asked, reaching for a comic book leaning against a photograph.

"Don't touch!" It came out a little louder than he'd meant, but he couldn't let her disturb anything, not now. "Sorry, I didn't mean to yell. He's in the middle. George is on the right and the other is James."

Charlie quickly drew back. "So you're the baby of the family." It was more of a statement of fact than a question.

"That's me, last on the list."

"Last, though certainly not least," Charlie amended with the merest quirk of her lips.

"Shouldn't you be getting back? Old man Crabtree said you were swamped."

"We are. It's okay, though. It's near the end of my shift and Mr. Crabtree was going to bring this one over himself, but I begged him to let me because you and I are such good pals." The words spilled out of her.

Here, Robert raised one skeptical brow. *"Good pals?* Not the words I'd use."

"Robert, this is bigger than any fat contest someone may have nudged a little to win."

Now his other brow went up, then he gave in. They'd been mortal enemies when Charlie had cheated. But she'd been there for him when he needed a friend before and he could certainly use a friend now. Robert knew she was right. It was time to let the past go. "Truce?" he offered

"More like a stalemate," she amended.

Robert touched the pendant around his neck. It was very warm and he felt an electric shock when his fingers grazed it. What was going on? He stood and, as if in a dream, walked to his dresser. He had the sudden urge to reread all the copies of *The Maple Leaf Kid* arrayed around Patrick's picture.

Then he shifted his gaze to George's grinning face.

His mind ticked over faster and faster. Maybe this was a test, like when George was shot down over France. He was supposed to have faith in the cosmic connection between the pendant, the comic books and his brothers. Captain Ice, his ace of the air, had shown Robert that everything would work out swell with the fly boys if he believed.

The comic had shown him what would happen, how the story would unfold and the happy ending. He thoughtfully traced the headline on the November edition of the Kid, remembering every word of the story.

Robert knew what he had to do.

CHAPTER TWENTY-FOUR

A CRACK IN THE UNIVERSE

ROBERT STOOD AT HIS DRESSER and saluted each of his brave heroes. "Troops, duty calls and I will answer!" His eyes shone with an inner light as he urgently turned to Charlie. "I have to go to Kreller's drugstore!"

She looked at him, obviously worried at his unexpected and irrational outburst.

"You've had bad news, Rob. Maybe you should hang fire a while. You know, take a breath." She searched for some way to calm her friend down. "You're sick and fevers can really mess with you. Why not sit for a minute? I could make you a cup of tea!"

Ignoring her, Robert strode to his closet and quickly found a pair of pants and a shirt. He was about to tear off his pyjamas when he saw Charlie's shocked expression.

"I don't have time for social niceties. Turn around or do whatever modesty says you should do when a guy is going to get dressed in front of you." He pulled so hard on his flannel top that the buttons flew in all directions. He didn't care. Yanking his shirt on, he reached for his trousers as he fumbled with the tie on the pajama pants.

"Yikes!" Charlie squeaked. "Will you please tell me what's going on?"

"No time to explain. I have to get to Kreller's – *now!*"

Charlie hesitated a fraction of a second and then he could see she had made her decision or, more accurately, her commitment.

"Okay, let's go, Wonder Weed!"

She threw him two previously worn socks she found lying on the floor, then rummaged in a pile of clothes on a chair for a heavy sweater. "It's cold outside. You'll need this."

They thumped downstairs and were out the front door before Robert's parents could protest.

"Grab your bike. I'll get mine from the garage. We'll rendezvous at the end of the alley!" Robert called as he disappeared behind of the house.

Pedalling hard and dodging traffic, Robert felt lightheaded as they raced for the drug store. Absently, he noticed how the snow seemed to be pouring out of the streetlight in a beam of gossamer white powder. He almost giggled as he barely missed a delivery van turning left in front of him. Tonight, he was on a mission, as surely as Sedna or Ice or the Kid. Everything depended on making it in time.

"It's after seven," Charlie called as they skidded to a halt in front of the store. "He's probably closed."

"Look, the lights are still on. He's in there." Robert leapt off his bike, letting it fall to the ground with a fender-bending crash.

He ran to the door and pounded on the glass. "Mr. Kreller! It's me, Robert Tourond! Let me in, please! Let me in!"

He wiped the pane with his glove, peering inside. Had the old druggist left the lights on and gone home?

A movement at the back of the store caught his eye. Robert hammered on the door again and this time Charlie joined him. The noise couldn't be ignored and soon, Mr. Kreller was coming toward them.

"What on earth is going on? Why are you making such a racket?" he asked, opening the door a crack.

"Mr. Kreller, did the December issue of *The Maple Leaf Kid* come in?" Robert pressed, skipping the niceties.

"Oh, for heaven's sake. Is this what the fuss is about? Comic books!" Mr. Kreller did not sound impressed as he opened the door wider and motioned them in. "Yes, yes, it finally came in, better late than never. That's still no reason to raise the dead. I'm sure buying one more comic book could have waited until tomorrow, Robert."

Charlie stood beside Robert. Her face told him she thought he was acting crazy.

"I need it now." Robert started walking toward the counter. "Where is it?"

"Hold your horses. I'll get it." The pharmacist moved past his agitated customer and retrieved a familiar brown paper bag. "Ten cents and it's yours."

It was then Robert realized he'd left in such a hurry he hadn't brought any money with him. He frantically searched the pockets on his trousers, but all he found was an old gum wrapper. Panic rose. He knew the store policy – no credit and there'd be no relaxing that rule this time. He wildly tore at his pockets once more, hoping he'd missed some hidden change.

Charlie reached out and calmly placed a dime on the counter. "Thank you for opening your store, Mr. Kreller. We won't keep you any longer." She took the bag and gave it to Robert, then pulled him toward the door. "Will you settle down?" she warned. "You're acting like a madman."

As they retrieved their bikes, Robert carefully tucked the bag under his sweater, not wanted to chance it getting wet. "I have to get home and read this right away."

"Ah, I figured that part out, Sherlock." Charlie shook her head as they started back.

At Robert's house, they raced upstairs to his room, passing his parents in the hallway. His father was on the telephone, probably talking to his grandparents and Katherine about the news. Robert could hear the tension in his father's voice as he spoke and couldn't help but notice the strain on his mother's face.

Once inside, he closed the door, saluted his brothers, then carefully smoothed out the covers on his bed before reverently placing the bag down. He took off his wet sweater, tossed it in the corner, then searched in his dresser drawer for the box of Eddy matches he'd stashed. Lighting the candle, he straightened the comic books next to each picture, making sure everything was absolutely perfect before returning to his bed.

Charlie stood quietly in the corner watching. She still had her uniform jacket on, and this she slowly unbuttoned and removed, the melting snow making a puddle on the floor.

Robert noted her respectful attitude and decided she must understand the importance of this ceremony. He took a breath and reached into the bag. With the utmost care, he removed the December issue of *The Maple Leaf Kid*.

He was rewarded with an explosion of colour and imagery. There was the Kid, being held in the clutches of two Gestapo guards while an SS officer aimed his Luger at our struggling hero. Towering above them was an ominous, cloud-shrouded medieval castle, complete with turrets and arrow slits in the crenellated stone walls. A reddish glow emanated from one tower room, like a beacon from hell.

Robert felt dizzy as he turned to the first page. He raked the panels, taking every detail in, reading each word and committing it to memory. The story was exciting, with the Maple Leaf Kid continuing to fight the enemy with his brain power and cunning. He was still in Italy and the Nazis were now hunting him as he was a known threat to the Third Reich – an enemy to be captured, tortured for his secrets, then slowly put to death by the foulest means.

The amulet around Robert's neck pulsed. He could feel his blood zinging through his veins as he read. The action continued to ramp up; the tension kept building. This was truly a door between the two worlds.

Blinking, Robert looked around at the Italian countryside. The air was sweetly scented and the olive groves were exactly as Patrick had described them. He felt the hot cobblestones under his feet as he ran toward the foreboding castle towering in the distance.

Sweating with effort, Robert climbed the ancient stone steps leading to the interior of the fortress. Ahead in the gloom, torches flickered, sending eerie shadows dancing across the walls. He saw the Nazis dragging the Maple Leaf Kid toward his doom.

Robert's eyes locked with the Kid's.

They both knew escape was impossible.

CHAPTER TWENTY-FIVE

STARDUST RESCUE

The Maple Leaf Kid had been captured and transported, but not to Gestapo headquarters in Rome. Instead, the diabolical brutes had spirited him to a secret fortress called Castello Della Morta, carved out of the jagged rock of the cliff itself, high in a remote area of the Italian mountains. Sinister, impregnable and so isolated no one could rescue the Kid. He was at the enemy's mercy, of which they had none.

The Kid was taken to an old storage room, high in a turret, and locked in with a meagre daily ration of maggoty food and a single cup of water. His captors wanted him to break the top-secret Allied communications code so they could intercept information. They'd steal Allied secrets and then send false messages to cause chaos. To motivate the Kid the Nazis had rounded up local villagers – if he didn't break the code soon, they'd start shooting their innocent hostages.

Our hero was in a jam. He already knew the secret code; he'd figured it out long ago. Although he had it, there was no way he would betray the Allies by giving it to the Nazis. He also couldn't allow the defenceless villagers to be slaughtered. He had to stall for time until he could get help.

It was then that the Kid noticed a stack of old radios stored in a corner of his tower cell. Ordinarily, they would be of no use, but the Kid was no ordinary prisoner. He set to work tearing apart the nonfunctioning devices and found what he was searching for – the crystal detectors. These, he knew, were made out of silicon carbide; carborundum. He retrieved the silicate, ground it up and, using his drinking water, made a paste. Grabbing the metal plate he ate his disgusting meals on, the Kid dipped his shirttail into the dark, gooey muck he'd created and then rubbed the bottom of the plate.

He continued rubbing the saucer with the silicon carbide. Suddenly a noise came from outside his door. He quickly hid everything.

"Ver ist your dish ?" the guard asked.

The Kid knew he had to be careful. If the soldier spotted the modification he'd made, there was no telling what they would do to him. He held the plate out like an urchin begging in the street, then wrinkled his nose. "Smells as good as it tastes." The guard slopped a ladle of vile brown gruel into the dish then left, locking the door securely.

Emptying the plate, the Kid went back to rubbing the bottom with the silicon carbide. It didn't take long before the metal shone like a mirror, which was exactly what the Maple Leaf Kid wanted. Moving to the arrow-slit windows, he spotted what he'd been praying for. There, at the bottom of the deep gorge, a small line of vehicles snaked its way along. It was a Canadian armoured column!

The heavy cloud bank broke and the sun shone in all its brilliant glory. Holding the plate out the narrow opening, the Kid proceeded to flash a message in Morse code to the trucks below, praying some bright Canadian trooper would scan the hilltops and spot his signal. Minutes later, returning flashes told him his message had been received and a rescue mission was coming. All he had to do was sit tight and wait.

But the Kid was out of time. He was hauled down to the courtyard where five villagers stood against the stone wall, a firing squad at the ready.

Waving his gun in the Kid's face, the cruel commandant

gave his ultimatum. "We discovered you already have the secret codes. If you don't give them to us now, these vorthless serfs vill be shot!"

The Kid stood fast. "Killing these innocent people will do you no good. I'll never betray my country!"

"Then you all die!" The officer grinned evilly.

The firing squad raised their rifles and the villagers clutched each other in terror. Before the fatal order could be given, *ka-BOOM!* The air was rent by a huge explosion! Canadian troops came storming through the smoking gates and the surprised Germans surrendered.

As usual, the Kid was modest as he accepted praise for his ingenuity. "All I did was signal with my polished plate. The Canadian troops saved the day."

"What did you use to make it so shiny?" asked the battle-hardened corporal.

"Silicon carbide I found in the detectors of some old radios. I guess you could say the Nazis gave me my means of escape."

"You can thank your lucky stars you found the stuff," the soldier said.

The Maple Leaf Kid laughed. "Lucky stars are exactly what did the trick. The most common form of silicon carbide is what we call *stardust!*"

Robert gasped. That was the clue – stardust! The universe was speaking and he would listen. He touched his own piece of fallen star and felt it hum.

"I know what's happened to Patrick," he said firmly. "He's been captured by the Germans and they're holding him in a secret location somewhere near Ortona."

"What on earth are you talking about?" Charlie asked, confused.

"Nothing *on earth* at all!" Robert laughed. "I know I'm right. The comic book has told me what to do. We have to get the army to send a rescue party to find Patrick."

Charlie's lips went into their hard line. He knew she was ready for battle.

"Robert, you're not going to sit there and tell me your stupid comic book is sending you secret messages *again!*"

"That's exactly what I'm telling you." He held up the new edition of *The Maple Leaf Kid*. "Don't you see? The Kid is telling me what happened to Patrick, like Ice did with George. The telegram said he is MIA, *missing* in action. The reason they can't find him is because he isn't where they expect him to be. He's being held in a secret location, an old castle or something. The comic book story is almost identical to what happened to Patrick. The Maple Leaf Kid was caught because the Nazis wanted to get information. Patrick's commanding officer sent him to capture a German soldier so the Canadian army could get information. Only Patrick ended up being the one taken instead." Robert jumped off the bed. "We have to tell my parents! They'll be thrilled!"

Charlie's face grew pink. "This is truly nuts!" She pointed at his dresser. "This, this *shrine* you have set up is not linking you to some creepy cosmos. *MIA* isn't some kind of get out of jail free card. We've delivered enough follow-up telegrams to know what's coming next. MIA means the soldier's dead and they haven't found his body because it was blown to bits or is lying in enemy-held territory!" She was livid now. "I'm sorry to be so brutal, but you need to hear the truth. You can't go to your parents and bleat out this insane story when they are dealing with...with *reality!* I'm sure *they* know what that telegram means."

Robert's temper exploded. He wouldn't listen to this traitor. "Shut up, Charlie! I'm telling you it's real. Patrick is not dead! He's being held prisoner and we can't let anyone, *especially* his family, give up on him."

He paced anxiously around the room. "I need the military to get in on this ASAP. I have to get them to organize a search party of all the castles and strongholds in the area where the Canadians were fighting."

He was like a runaway train – Charlie had to put the brakes on. "I'll tell you what," she said. "Tomorrow is Friday. I'll ditch school and come over then we can try to figure something out together, only you have to promise you won't say anything about this to your parents. Deal?"

It was late and Robert could see the logic in this, however hard it would be to wait. The good thing was delaying would give him time to come up with a workable plan he could take to the army. "Okay, okay, deal."

As he picked up her damp uniform jacket, something occurred to Robert. "Are you going to ride all the way to Bowness now?" Outside the window, the snow was coming down harder.

"Yeah. I'll be fine." She didn't sound very sure.

"Come on. You need a ride and not on Big Betsy."

"This is not the time to ask your father for a lift home, Rob."

Her lips were doing the thin-line thing again and Robert knew there'd be no budging her. "Who said anything about asking my dad?"

They went downstairs to find his mother on the couch and his father on the phone.

"...yes, that's all we know. Helen is taking it very hard." His father looked up as Robert and Charlie walked into the room. "Here's Robert now," he held the receiver out. "It's Kathryn."

Robert took the phone. "Hi Katy."

"Robbie, oh sweetheart, I am so sorry to hear this news. I wish I was there to help in some way."

He knew she was being comforting, but she didn't understand there was no reason to worry and he couldn't explain now. "Don't worry, cuz. Everything is going to be fine as frog's hair." He must have sounded too cheery because Kathryn immediately switched to her lawyer's voice, all business.

"Robert, why would you say that? You do understand what this could mean? I know how close you and Patrick are."

He dismissed her grave tone. "Like I said, everything's going to be okay. Gotta go." He handed the receiver back to his father. "I'll be back in a while."

There was no argument, and Robert figured that was due to the seriousness of what was going on. If only they knew what had really happened to Patrick.

Mr. Glowinski was, as usual, working in his shop when Robert knocked at the door. "Mr. G, could I ask you a huge favour?"

"Of course, what you need, Robcio?"

Robert noticed the big man was wearing his talisman, which made him feel surprisingly close to his neighbour. They shared a special bond. "Charlie's on her bike. It's late and snowing so hard, I was hoping you could give her a ride home. The only catch is, she lives way out in Bowness."

Mr. Glowinski immediately put down the screwdriver he was holding. "Sure, sure. No problem. I get coat and car keys. You bring bike."

They met him in front of his house with the bike and he jammed it in the rumble seat of the two-door car.

"This is my new joy," Mr. Glowinski said proudly. "I just buy her."

Robert eyed the vintage car. "What is it?"

"This 1929 Chevrolet International AC Sport Coupe, with the new in-line six cylinders," he announced like an ad from *The Star Weekly*.

Charlie didn't seem impressed and Robert chalked it up to her being a girl and not interested in true guy stuff. "She's a beauty."

They piled into the car and Robert was acutely aware of Charlie crushed up against him on the bench seat.

"Sorry, Wonder Weed. Mr. G needs room to shift the stick."

"I don't think Robcio mind much," Mr. Glowinski said confidently.

When they pulled up to Charlie's house, the lights were on and Robert could see a party was in full swing. Music blared into the street as the screen door opened and two revelers lurched onto the porch.

"Oh, great." Charlie fumed as she clambered out of the car. 'It's going to be another late one."

Mr. Glowinski retrieved her bike. "You sure you be okay, miss?" He eyed the drunken scene spilling out of the house.

"No problem. The cops should show up in about fifteen minutes and shut it down."

Robert unexpectedly felt very protective. "You could come back with us, Charlie."

"You don't need any strangers bunking at your place right now, Wonder Weed. Besides, this will all be over soon. See you tomorrow." She took the bike from Mr. Glowinski. "Thank you for the ride, Mr. G. I really didn't want to bike home in the snow."

She wheeled her bicycle around the corner of the narrow shotgun house and disappeared.

"I think she not worst enemy anymore." Mr. Glowinski commented as he turned the car back toward home.

"Maybe not...for now." Robert allowed as he rolled plans around in his head.

Charlie was, well, she was Charlie, and he was getting used to her tough attitude and moodiness. Maybe that's what all girls were like; maybe he'd never understand any of them. Whatever the case, understanding females was a problem for another day.

Right now, Patrick was his main focus. His brother needed his help! The question was, how was he going to convince his parents and the army to believe in his comic book war?

CHAPTER TWENTY-SIX

ACTION HEROES

THE NEXT DAY, GRIEF covered the Tourond house like a dark blanket. His father was a statue, standing by the kitchen sink holding a mug of tea as he stared blindly at the snowy back yard. Robert made breakfast and watched him, noticing his father never once took a drink.

After washing his dishes, Robert was on his way to his room when there was a knock at the front door. He opened it to find Charlie standing on the porch. Her over-sized black ear muffs made her look like a little kid. She was in civvies; men's boots that didn't fit, denim work pants and a threadbare green cotton jacket that wouldn't have been warm on a July day.

"Hey, Rob. How's things?" she asked, stepping inside.

"Gloomy, which is why I need to share my master plan with the folks. I have to get the Kid first." He hustled upstairs then returned with the comic book and a navy pea coat. "I dug this out last night after I got home," he said, handing it to her. "It was Patrick's, then mine, but I've outgrown it. It's warm and the price is great: ten cents. Oh, wait a minute, I owe you a dime from last night at Kreller's, so I guess we could consider it square if you wanted the jacket." He made the bargain knowing she wouldn't like charity.

"The comic was your Christmas present, a couple of days

early. If you insist on making it about money, I suppose you could consider it payment in full. I have to tell you though, I got the better deal," she teased. "Thanks, Rob."

He knew she must have been frozen on the ride over, and felt glad she now had a much warmer coat to battle the frigid temperatures. He also kind of liked the idea of her wearing his old jacket.

"Come on. Wait till you hear what I came up with." Together they went into the living room where his parents were now seated together on the sofa. They desperately clung to one another, as if in a lifeboat lost at sea.

"Mom, Dad, you remember Charlie from work?"

Instantly, fear sprang into his mother's face. "You don't have another telegram for us?"

"No, Mum, she's not working now. Charlie's here because she's a friend." Robert quickly reassured his mother. "Do you remember when George was shot down?"

"Of course we do, son. What's it got to do with Patrick?" His father's tone let Robert know he was in no mood for games.

"I told you about the comic book connection and how the story mirrored what was happening to George?"

"And I told you it was all nonsense and nothing but coincidence."

"The same thing is happening again, only with Patrick. I have the new edition of *The Maple Leaf Kid*, he's assigned to Patrick and the Kid was in Italy, too. Then he was captured by the Germans and held in a secret fortress called Castello Della Morta. That's what's happened to Patrick. He's been captured and we need to go to the military so they can find the castle and get him back." He laid the comic on the coffee table, open so his parents could see the fantastic last page with the incredible rescue.

His father stood. "Do you know what Castello Della Morta means? It translates into *Castle of Death*. Are you telling me your brother is being held in an Italian castle called *Death*?"

"No, it was the name in the comic. Who knows what the name of the one Patrick's in is called."

"You actually want me to go to the army and tell them this ridiculous story. They'd lock us all up and throw away the key!" Robert felt his frustration building, but tried to be patient. "I know you and Mum don't know much about what goes on behind the scenes to support the war. Me, I've been keeping up with all the news. Sending troops in to find one lost soldier is not crazy. It would be the story of the century for the army. The propaganda alone would be worth the rescue effort."

His father turned on him. "*We* don't know what goes on? What do you think your mother and I do? We support our fighting boys each and every day."

Robert was at the end of his patience. The man just didn't understand the big picture. "Dad, making crop fertilizer is not exactly front line war effort and Mum's victory garden and knitting club won't save many lives." He didn't want to belittle his parents help, but he couldn't see how they thought they were really having an impact on the fighting overseas.

His father grew very still. "Is that what you think I do, make fertilizer? Robert, I make ammonium nitrate; it's used in explosives! It's in aerial bombs and depth charges. I think I contribute a lot to the 'front line war effort.'" He was building up a full head of steam now. "As for your mother – she's a war-effort dynamo. She organizes drives from metal to paper, bringing in tons of raw materials that are turned into planes and bullets. She also supervises making ditty bags for our boys so they at least have a few comforts from home. Did you know your mother personally runs this area's program that supplies Red Cross war relief packages? Those packages help thousands of our men who are enduring hell in prisoner-of-war camps overseas." He took a breath. "You need to keep up with the news here at home, young man." He sat back down next to his wife. "We're not going to entertain any silly notions you have about comic books telling us where your brother is. He's out there, wounded maybe, and I know he's trying to get back to us. He'll make it. He has to."

His mother had been sitting stoically on the couch, but she

rose now and walked to Robert. He waited for a blast from her too. Unexpectedly, she reached out and gently touched his cheek. "I know how hard it's been on you to have all your brothers gone overseas. You must have felt deserted, like they left you behind while they went off to have fabulous adventures. Maybe your dad and I have been busy with our war work and we, too, have left you out. For that, I'm sorry, son. I've seen how much you've grown up these past months. We'll get through this and then we'll talk, but for now, we have to face reality, no matter how hard, and we'll face it together." She gave him a quick kiss, then went to sit next to his father

Robert was speechless. His mother had never said anything like this before nor had she ever said she was sorry about anything. It made him feel unexpectedly close to her.

And she was being very reasonable, so why couldn't she see what was so obvious? The Kid had shown them what was coming. All they had to do was believe.

Arguing was useless. "I know I'm right. Come on, Charlie."

He grabbed the Kid and stormed upstairs to his room with Charlie close behind. Once they were inside, he closed the door. "I have a plan, but I have to warn you, it involves a little subterfuge. Are you coming with me?"

"If I don't watch out for you, you'll end up in the hoosegow for sure."

"Hoosegow?"

"You know, the big house, the slammer, the calaboose!" She wiggled her eyebrows at him. "I've got two brothers up the river right now."

"You could be joining them if things don't go right." Robert started unbuttoning his shirt.

"Holy smokes! What is it with you and undressing, Wonder Weed?" She turned her back to him.

"Let's go." When she turned around, Robert was in full uniform, including his cap, which was set at a rakish angle. He'd smudged something over his lip giving the appearance of an eleven o'clock shadow, like he'd forgotten to shave his mustache.

"What's with the fake fuzz?" she asked.

He tucked the Kid into his satchel as they left the room. "It's part of my disguise, so I appear older and more responsible. Like someone who should be listened to." He pulled on his boots and gloves while Charlie slipped into her pea coat. He appraised her in his old jacket. "Say, that suits you way better than it did me."

"Not freezing my butt suits me, Wonder Weed. Where are we going?"

"David's taking on Goliath."

They sped off on their bikes with Robert leading the way. A Chinook was blowing in and the temperatures were sky rocketing. Soon, it would be downright balmy.

They stopped in front of a pair of impressive gates with *Currie Barracks* artfully scrolled across the top. "Follow my lead," Robert instructed as they pedaled up to the guard house.

"State your business." The private at the gate obviously excelled at doing his job.

"Telegram delivery." Robert pointed at the company crest on his cap and tried to make his voice sound businesslike and mature.

"Let's see it," the guard demanded.

Robert took an envelope out of his satchel.

"Give it here," the soldier ordered.

Robert snatched the envelope back. "I can't relinquish the document without proper clearance." This sounded suitably official. "It would help if you could tell me where to find the addressee."

"What's his name?"

Robert pretended to read the name on the telegram. "Squadron Leader Aberdeen."

"Oh, yeah, he'll be one of those fly boys with the Number 3 Service Flying Training School." He explained how to get to the office through the maze of buildings comprising the base. "Who's the civilian?" The private pointed at Charlie.

"Trainee. Sanctioned by the Head Telegrapher to accompany me." Here Robert leaned in over his handlebars and spoke under his breath. "I'm trying to teach her the ropes, but she's a little slow and needs all the practice she can get." His tone was conspiratorial.

The soldier nodded knowingly. "Yeah. My sister is helpless without a man to show her how it's done." He raised the wooden barricade. "Good luck."

"*A little slow?*" Charlie growled as they pedaled away.

"I got us in, didn't I?" Robert grinned as he sped ahead of her.

THEY WAITED WHILE the clerk went to speak to Squadron Leader Aberdeen, who looked surprised when they were ushered into his office.

"What's this all about? Something happened to George I don't know about?" He sat back in his chair.

"No, sir. George is fine. It's my other brother, Patrick. He's with the Loyal Edmonton Regiment at Ortona."

The squadron leader sat up. "The Eddies have been hit hard. If your brother is with them, he's earning his paycheque for sure."

Robert plunged on. "Sir, I need your help. We received a telegram saying Patrick's missing in action. I know what everyone thinks, but he's alive, I'm sure of it. He's being held hostage by the Nazis, in a castle somewhere near Ortona. I need to convince the army to send a reconnaissance patrol to find him and bring him home. You were so kind and helpful when George went down in France, I'm hoping we can work together to save Patrick."

Robert paused to watch the squadron leader for any hint of disbelief, but the guy had a poker face. "There can't be many castles around, which means it should be possible. His life depends on it. Once they figure out he doesn't have any sensitive information, they'll send him to a POW camp or kill him."

"How do you know all this, Robert?" The squadron leader asked calmly.

Here Robert hesitated. He knew how this was going to

sound. "I kind of have a pipeline of information about my brothers. It's hard to believe, so please, hear me out." He explained about the comic books and how they foretold what was happening overseas. He talked about how Ice had mirrored George and took out his copy of *The Maple Leaf Kid* to show the squadron leader. Once he was done, he sat back and waited.

The officer wasn't convinced. Robert could see he had lost credibility and along with it, his one hope of saving Patrick.

"I know how this sounds, sir," Charlie jumped in. "But I've seen and heard a lot about this and maybe there is something going on here. Has anything ever happened to you that couldn't be explained and seemed completely irrational, but turned out to be true? Rob's cosmic connection is like that. I believe him, Squadron Leader Aberdeen, and his brother's life depends on you taking a leap of faith."

There was a long silence, with only the ticking of a clock to mark the painful passage of time. Finally the battle-hardened pilot spoke.

"Comic book heroes who take care of your brothers? Even if I believe you, no one else will. It's Christmas Eve, why don't you leave it with me and I'll see what I can do." He stood up. "I can't promise anything, however, I'll make some inquiries. I will tell you this – no one wants to leave a man behind."

"This is a great start. Thank you, sir." Robert patted the pendant tucked under his shirt. He knew this was the best he could hope for and at least the machine was in motion.

They rode away in high spirits. Robert had faith there would be positive results before long. He stole a glance at Charlie. "That was something, what you did back there. Stepping up to the plate, I mean."

A sliver of a smile appeared on her face. "It's not often I find someone who's crazier than me and now it's official. You're on record to the military about believing in this, this..."

"Comic book war," Robert filled in. "And I'll put my superheroes up against Hitler any day."

"I'll take Jimmy Stewart, Cary Grant or Humphrey Bogart,"

Charlie said, listing her favourite actors. "Those are heroes worth my money."

From her voice, he knew these Hollywood stars were important. She'd mentioned movies a couple of times as they waited for deliveries, and Robert understood what they meant to her. He escaped into his comic books to keep sane and he suspected she did the same thing with movies. He had an idea. "So are you doing anything this afternoon? Maybe your family does something special on Christmas Eve?"

She snorted. "You mean besides getting drunk as a pack of thirsty skunks? Nope, can't say my dance card is filled."

"You want to go see Bogart's movie *Casablanca*, with me? It's playing at the Grand." Then he felt stupid for asking – what if she thought it was a date? "Um, you see, I don't want to go home right now and I bet you don't either."

She slid a sidelong glance at him. "You buy the popcorn?"

He pretended to think about this. "Yeah, I suppose."

"You've got a deal, Wonder Weed."

Then he remembered. They both had to work. "I forgot. We have to deliver those wonderful three-cent telegrams."

"Nope. I called Mr. Crabtree and explained everything, and he said under the circumstances, we could have the day off with his blessing. He's going to borrow a couple of boys from another office for the day. I'd say that's sweet as sugar without the flies."

THEY SPENT THE AFTERNOON watching the film, and Robert had to admit that Humphrey Bogart as Rick, the American nightclub owner in Nazi-ridden Casablanca, was great. When they left the theatre, Robert snuck a peek at Charlie. She was happy and sappy all at the same time.

"Wasn't it divine? Isn't Bogey dreamy?" she sighed.

Robert almost laughed. He wasn't used to seeing Charlie like this. She sounded like some starstruck teenager, which, he guessed she was. "It was okay," he said casually.

"Are you kidding? *Casablanca* is brilliant! Besides, I saw your eyeballs glued to the silver screen, so don't try to blow it off as some third-rate flick, *Wonder Weed.*"

He remembered how long ago, he'd been upset at his nickname. Now he liked it. She was the only one who called him that.

"Okay, I admit, I liked how Rick fought the Nazis in his own way, and did the right thing, even if it meant giving up Ilsa."

"Me, too," Charlie agreed. "And I loved the scene in the bar where Ilsa asks Sam the piano player for *As Time Goes By.* It really got to me." She looked wistful. "Say, I've never heard of Ingrid Bergman, have you?"

"She's from Sweden." He liked showing off his insider knowledge to her, even if he had only found out from the girl behind the candy counter when he'd bought the popcorn.

Charlie was bubbling now. "My favourite part was the way Rick said, 'Here's looking at you, kid,' when he said goodbye to Ilsa. You could just tell what he really meant."

Robert was lost. He'd thought the line was catchy, but didn't guess there was a hidden meaning. "Uh, it meant, 'See ya, Ilsa, you Norwegian babe'."

She gave him an exasperated look. "He was telling her he loved her. He was still smitten."

"Smitten?"

She bumped him with her shoulder. "You know, head over heels."

"Oh. *Smitten.*"

They walked on together in companionable silence.

He had to admit, *Casablanca* was a really great movie, especially the ending. Rick shoots the Nazi creep, Strasser, then sends Ilsa and her husband to safety, even though he really wants her to stay with him. In the closing scene, Captain Renault – the French cop – and Rick are walking into the fog and Rick says, "Louie, I think this is the beginning of a beautiful friendship." It was the best last line of any movie he had ever seen in his entire life.

He wondered if this was the beginning of a beautiful friendship between him and Crazy Charlie Donnelly. She'd stuck beside him and hadn't bailed out when things got tough. He liked that. He also understood her better her now, and it only made him like her more.

Too soon, they arrived at their bikes.

"I've got to finish my Christmas shopping on the way home," he admitted.

"Nothing like leaving it to the last minute." Charlie laughed. "Christmas shopping for my dear parents is easy. I buy a bottle of rye from a bootlegger, stick a bow on it and call it done."

Robert didn't comment as Charlie pulled on her mitts.

He waited until she was ready to leave, then Robert turned to his friend. "Have a good Christmas, or as good as you can, Charlie. And if I don't see you, remember...we'll always have Paris."

Charlie laughed at his Bogart imitation.

Smiling, Robert jumped on his bike and pedaled away.

CHAPTER TWENTY-SEVEN

HOMECOMING

CHRISTMAS 1943 WAS an understandably sombre affair at the Tourond house. Robert's mother tried to make it as normal as possible, which would have been hard to do at the best of times with three sons away from home, but now, with one of them waiting for rescue, it was verging on the impossible.

Robert had bought his mother a bottle of Evening in Paris perfume. She loved the present and said she would keep the elegant blue bottle, even when the perfume was gone. For his father, he'd bought something unusual.

"What's this?" his dad asked, unwrapping the gift.

Weeks ago, Robert had bought his father a new football so they could do something together, something father-and-son like. Now he wasn't sure it was the right thing to have done. His dad had never seemed interested before.

"I thought we could toss it around, once the weather warms up, you know, if you want." Robert felt awkward, maybe because he and his father had never played catch or kicked a football, not just the two of them. He hoped there was still time.

His father rolled the ball around, then threw it to his son. "I think that would be a good idea, a very good idea. Thanks, son. This might be one of the best presents I've ever had."

Robert chucked the ball back. "If the Chinook stays, we

could try it out tomorrow."

"I'd better warn you, son, my spiral's still got a heck of a punch." His dad spun the end of the football on his finger tip.

"We'll see about that, old man..." His father scowled and Robert thought he'd gone too far, but then his dad chuckled.

"Your old man may surprise you yet, kid."

That was one surprise Robert would look forward to.

OVER THE NEXT WEEK, Robert confirmed that patience wasn't his strong suit as he waited for news about Patrick. He convinced himself the aggravation would all be worth it when Squadron Leader Aberdeen showed up with his good news and the celebrating commenced. Every day, he walked into Mr. Crabtree's office and one shake of the telegrapher's head told him nothing had arrived there either.

Robert wished his parents would believe him so they wouldn't be put through the agony of waiting, fearing the worst. His mother was a basket case and his father not much better. Somehow, they did what Touronds do best – they soldiered on.

"Did your other pen-and-ink heroes arrive with news no one knows yet?" Charlie asked as they walked into the office together after returning from a delivery run.

"It's a weird thing. Neither Sedna nor Ice have shown up. Even Mr. Kreller hasn't any idea why." Robert had put it down to wartime supplies always drying up – maybe the comic book printers had run out of ink or something. He wasn't worried, at least not too much.

Saturday was New Year's Day and still there was no news about Patrick. Robert decided this was good. He was sure the army was scaling some tower wall at that very moment.

The week before, he'd had another telegram delivery to the Polish businessman and had asked him what would be the right treat for New Year's in Poland. The answer had been *faworkowe róze*, a delicious pastry. Then he'd cajoled his mother into making it for Mr. Glowinski as a surprise. Robert wanted 1944 to be a better year for his neighbour and hoped the tasty treat would be a good start.

"This nice, Robcio. If my Marta here, she would be very happy and say thank you for kind thoughts and delicious present." He shook Robert's hand formally then accepted the gift . "Any words on your brother?"

"Not yet. I'm sure news is going to come any day now."

"*Tak, tak,*" his neighbour agreed. "Good you come. I forgot to give you this before." He passed Robert a folded piece of paper with *Robcio* scrawled across the front.

Inside was the last fragment of his meteorite.

"I thought you should have it, in case."

It was fashioned exactly like Robert's original, fancy metal work and all, only smaller with a finer chain. "Thanks Mr. G. It's a great back-up in case anything ever happens to mine." He touched his pendant, reassuring himself it was safe. Even the thought of losing his star made him shiver.

"Back-up...maybe." The soft-spoken man smiled knowingly. "Come. We have tea and one of these delicious pastries, *tak.*"

"*Tak,*" Robert agreed.

He'd never been inside his neighbour's house before. He took in the sparse furnishings. There were few luxuries, none in fact. Then Robert saw something that drew him closer. In pride of place on the mantle was a small, worn black-and-white photograph. He peered closely, but it was hard to see the image on the cracked surface.

"That my family. I have picture with me when I escape. Only one." Mr. G poured them tea.

Robert realized he could never imagine what this man had lived through. It showed him you could overcome any tragedy, with a little help from your friends.

"You had a beautiful family, Mr. G."

"We friends, Robcio. You call me Teddy. It short for Tadeusz."

Robert held up his mug of tea. "Here's to a great 1944, Teddy." They clinked cups and talked for a long while. Teddy told him about his engineering work and how busy he was with the fix-it shop and Robert explained about seeing *Casablanca* with Charlie and how much they both liked the movie. When he finally went home, he felt very good about his visit with his friend, Teddy Glowinski.

IT WAS NEARING the end of the first full week of January when Robert stopped by Kreller's drugstore.

"Hi, Mr. Kreller. I know last month's Sedna and Ice still haven't shown up and January's will be here soon, but if the December issues ever do come in, I'd like everything, old and new."

Mr. Kreller put away a large bottle of pills on a shelf before facing Robert. "Actually, Robert, I got a letter from the distributor today. The company that publishes *Sedna of the Sea*, *Captain Ice* and *The Maple Leaf Kid* has gone out of business. There won't be any more of those particular comics."

Robert was stunned. "All three? They're gone?"

"I'm afraid so, lad."

Panic squeezed the breath out of him and a rushing in his ears made it hard to hear what Mr. Kreller said next.

"So, do you want me to keep any others for you? *Captain Canuck* or *Canada Jack*? Maybe *Nelvana of the Northern Lights*?"

Robert couldn't speak. Turning, he walked out of the store and went home. Once in his room, he blindly stood at his dresser. He didn't know what to say to his brothers. How could this happen? And what did it mean for George, James and Patrick?

Sleep didn't come for the next few nights as Robert imagined all sorts of calamities happening to his brothers. When letters finally did arrive from George and James, he was afraid to open them. In the end, he couldn't stand it and he read his brothers' letters. Strangely, everything was fine, apart from their worry about Patrick. George had been out on some exciting missions and James had several funny stories about his Home Guard pals. Nothing else. No terrible tragedies. No pain and blood.

The following week, Robert was at his locker when Charlie hurried up.

"Any news?" she asked, unbuttoning her pea coat.

"Have patience. It takes time to knock down a castle fortress."

"I'm sure it does. You may as well know now, I'm no good at waiting."

She took off her toque and shook out her hair. "Can I come to your place after work? It's my birthday and for my parents, that's as good an excuse as any for a party. Some of their hillbilly friends are coming over and I'd rather not be there."

"I know it's your birthday and sure, you can come over."

She gave him a quizzical look. "You know it's my birthday?"

He hesitated a second, then furrowed his brow like he was remembering something. "I, uh, I might have seen it on your job application."

Charlie crossed her arms and waited for more information.

"Hey, 'know your enemy' and, at the time, you were the very definition of an enemy. I was gathering intel. Are you sure you don't want to spend it with your family?"

Her hard expression and thin lips said it all. This turn of events fit in with Robert's plans perfectly. "Then it's settled. You'll come for supper. It's Call It Delicious or Else Spam night."

Charlie giggled. "It sounds wonderful."

Work went well, with both of them having a high-paying delivery, and by the time they wended their way back to Robert's house they were ravenous.

"Even Spam sounds good to me right now," Robert called.

He was about to turn down his alley, when something on the street in front of his house caught his eye.

It was a car, a familiar car. It was Squadron Leader Aberdeen's.

Robert's heart leapt as he pumped up his speed. They must have freed Patrick! He was safe and coming home! Charlie had spotted the car, too, and was right behind him as they wheeled up to his garage and raced to the house.

Barging through the back door, Robert ran to the living room with Charlie following breathlessly behind. He could hardly wait to hear the good news.

His parents looked up as he burst into the living room. "I told you!" he laughed. "Didn't I tell you he was being held prisoner!"

It was then Robert saw Squadron Leader Aberdeen holding an old Métis sash.

His mother was crying. More disturbing than this, so was his father. Robert had never seen his father cry before and it scared him. "What's happened?"

"Robert, your brother, he..." His father took a shaky breath. "Your brother died in action. They found him near where his patrol was ambushed. He was killed by a grenade and the force of the explosion blew off his identification tags so they didn't know it was him."

Robert couldn't speak. This wasn't true! It couldn't be.

The Squadron Leader took a step toward him. "When you came to see me, I contacted a padre attached to the Loyal Edmonton Regiment deployed at Ortona. He looked into Patrick's case and discovered what happened. Once they had a positive identification, they asked me to notify the family and sent Patrick's personal effects." The flying officer paused. "He was wearing the sash when they found him. There was a note in his belongings." He handed Robert a worn piece of paper.

Mon frere,

If you have this, then things have gone badly. I need you to be strong for the family, especially Mum.

When you sent that old sash, I thought it was daft, but you know something, Robert, it made me feel better to wear it. Less afraid. I knew you were all rooting for me back home. I hope it will do the same for you.

Always remember, you are the best brother a guy could ever have.

I love you.

See you in the stars,

Patrick

Robert stared at the words. *See you in the stars.* His hand started to shake.

This wasn't right. This wasn't what he'd been waiting for. The Maple Leaf Kid was never wrong.

He remembered how he'd wanted Patrick to give him the family relic because of all the memories it held, all the history. He did want the old sash, but not like this, not taken from his dead brother's body.

"No. This is impossible," he said emphatically.

The Squadron Leader voice was firm. "There is no mistake. I'm sorry, son."

Robert shook his head, denying the words, denying the reality. "They're wrong. Patrick has been captured. He's alive, in a castle, waiting for us to rescue him. The Kid wouldn't lie to me! He wouldn't!" He saw the faces of his parents, their unendurable grief and the terrible truth reflected in their eyes.

Robert's world splintered. The walls of the room cracked open. Images from his favourite episodes of *Captain Ice, Sedna of the Sea* and his friend, *The Maple Leaf Kid* flashed before him, burst like fireworks, then faded in a trail of dancing sparks. Everything dissolved in front of his eyes, melting like candles in a fire. He couldn't breathe and panic welled up in him.

"It was all a lie!" he whispered, the realization exploded in his mind.

Dropping the note, Robert stumbled from the room and into the night. Dead. *Patrick was dead.*

Jumping on his bicycle, he rode away as fast as he could. He had no idea where he was going. All he knew for certain was he had to escape.

He rode blindly, through stoplights, down alleys until, gasping, he came to a stop at the base of the water tower. His water tower. His safe haven.

Scrambling up the ladder, Robert threw himself into a sheltered corner and hid his face from the world. He hurt so badly. Every fibre ached and he didn't know how to stop it. He was sure he was going to die.

Suddenly, arms were around him and he was gazing into gla-cier-blue eyes.

"If my worlds had been torn apart, this is where I would have come, too." Charlie explained softly.

She folded him into her embrace and this time, he let her hold him as they rocked silently back and forth. Now the tears came and Robert was powerless to stop them. He wept for all he had shared with his brother and all he would never share.

After a long while, his sobbing stopped and they sat together, neither saying a word, as they watched the fathomless night drift by.

Finally Charlie broke the silence. "Do you know why I needed the telegram job so badly? Why I cheated on the fat con-test and scratched for every delivery I could get?"

Robert shook his head.

"Because I'm leaving home. I'm moving to Sacred Heart Convent."

This caught Robert's attention and he sat up.

"A convent? Charlie, are you sure that's what you want to do with your life?"

"Don't be a sap. I'm not nun material. I'm going to St. Mary's Girls School and will be boarding at Sacred Heart Convent."

"What about your parents? What will they say?" Robert wiped his nose on his sleeve.

"I don't care. Remember I said I didn't like their hillbilly friends? On my last birthday, one of them thought I was old enough to be his new girlfriend. I had to stab the jerk to con-vince him I wasn't interested."

"You killed a man!" Robert was shocked.

"No, Wonder Weed. I stabbed him in the arm with a big old fork. He got the message. I decided then and there to get out. It's taken me a while to get enough money to escape."

Robert thought about the last months with Charlie. He had no idea what she'd been going through. He knew she'd had it hard, but had never dreamed of how terrible it really was. "Can I ask you something?"

"Shoot," she said.

"Despite being stuck with Old Betsy, you always managed to beat me on deliveries. How did you pull it off? "

"Because, Wonder Weed, I spent years and years running all over Calgary. I know every short cut, back alley and vacant lot there is. I simply rode my sneaky routes instead of running them."

"Another of life's mysteries explained."

The city lights twinkled in the cold night air as they huddled together.

"Rob," Charlie cleared her throat. "I don't know what to say about Patrick, except, I'm here for you." She bumped him. "I guess I'll always be here for you."

He took in all that this meant and all it implied. "Ditto."

They sat in silence a while longer, enjoying the peace. Then Robert spoke up, a lingering trace of bitterness in his voice.

"I was so sure my comic book stories were identical to what my brothers told me in their letters. They were my cosmic connection and nothing could hurt my brothers with their superhero guardians watching over them. How could I have been so wrong?"

"You were worried about your brothers, Rob, so worried you looked for any way you could to keep them safe. That says something about how close you were."

Robert shook his head. "I think if I reread them now, I'd say the letters and my comics had a few things sort of the same, but that's all. Maybe my comic book adventures changed how I read my brothers' stories. Comics were like an obsession. I was fooling myself."

She held his eyes with hers. "You love those comic books and there's nothing wrong with that. They tell great tales of imaginary heroes fighting imaginary villains. Don't you see – that's exactly what your brothers are doing – they're fighting the biggest super villain of all time but they're doing it for real. You're brothers are actual superheroes."

Robert sighed, then smiled weakly. "I guess you're right. It so happens their jobs coincide with a storyline that has been in every comic book since the beginning of time: good guy versus bad guy." He stretched his legs out, leaning back against the water tower and thought about his comic book war. "Maybe I imagined more in them than was really there, like I imagined I had some sort of super luck after finding the meteorite." He touched his talisman. It was quiet now, and Robert wondered if the magic was gone from it, or if there had ever been any magic in the first place. But when he thought of how much had happened since he'd found his star, he couldn't quite bring himself to believe it was only a pebble that had been floating around for millions of years in the cold, empty darkness.

"Hey, you weren't the only one imagining things." Charlie leaned back against the tower next to him. "I thought I was on some kind of wild lucky streak, too. Managing to fix the fat race without being caught and then Crabtree giving me the job despite the fact I was a girl."

"Yeah, I suppose it would seem like you were some kind of whiz kid. You were sure wrong about that." She ignored his zinger.

Robert went on, "I feel so bad for my parents and my brothers. Everything's going to change now. I'm changed now. I thought fighting over there was the best thing ever. But it's not a comic book adventure. Men die in war. Sons die in war. Brothers die in war." He felt an indescribable ache in every cell of his body. "I don't know what I'm going to do without him, Charlie. He was something special, you know. The best brother ever and I'm just a chump."

Charlie patted his leg. "Don't sell yourself short. You helped me when I needed a pal who knew someone with a fix-it shop."

"Yeah, I guess I did ride in on my white horse, even if it was actually a green bike and Mr. G did an amazing job with Big Betsy. I could hardly keep up."

Robert's mind went to another memory of his neighbour – that awful night in Mr. Glowinski's garage when his friend had come so close to extinguishing his own life. Teddy Glowinski had said he would change anything, *even reality*, to save his loved ones. Robert now understood exactly what that meant.

He flashed to something he'd planned for Charlie. Was it only hours and not years ago that he'd come up with his brilliant idea? Reaching into his jacket, he pulled out a small box. "Happy birthday, Charlene."

She took the box and opened it. Inside was a pendant that matched his own. "It's a piece of my meteorite." Robert now understood Mr. G's knowing smile when he'd handed the third pendant over. The delicate interstellar jewel had Charlie Donnelly's name written all over it. His very wise neighbour had seen that long before Robert did.

Gazing up at the night sky, Robert thought of Patrick and how they'd both seen this miracle gift fall. He imagined his brother up there now, watching over him, and saluted. *See you in the stars.*

"Did I tell you Patrick and I both saw a brilliant shooting star on the same night? I think this is it."

Charlie touched the tiny fragment of a mystery bigger than both of them, then she put the necklace on. It glimmered in the moonlight, almost as if it had a light of its own. "It's beautiful. And, Rob..."

"Yes?"

"I like *Charlie* better."

Robert turned to her and smiled, and then said, in his best Bogart voice, "Here's looking at you, *Charlie*."

And at that precise moment, both Charlie and Robert felt a warm tingling coming from the small fragment of the fallen star each of them wore.

EPILOGUE

———

SMOKING AND IN RUINS, THE ENEMY PLANE FELL FROM THE DARKENING SKY. WAGGLING HIS WINGS IN VICTORY AT LAST, OUR HERO BANKED HIS BATTERED LITTLE FIGHTER. THEN, WITH A SMILE AND A WAVE, HE FLEW INTO THE HEART OF THE WELCOMING SUN.

The Comic Book War

As a writer, I have done research on many different topics to make sure every detail is right in my books. For this one, however, I did take some literary licence with a few historical facts. For those readers who like having all the facts, here's what you should know.

TELEGRAPH DELIVERY

During the war, many young men were employed as telegram delivery boys, but few, if any, girls were part of this cadre. The ladies' talents were usually applied to sending and receiving the telegrams that the boys delivered. After a short period, it was decided that delivering military telegrams with their usually bad news was too hard for young people and that unenviable chore was given to adults.

POSTAL DELIVERY

In my story, Robert thinks about how irregular military mail delivery is, but letters are still arriving regularly from Robert's brothers. In actual fact, during World War II, mail from the front would have taken much longer to reach families back in Canada. However, to keep the plot rolling, I had to have those letters!

CANADIAN COMIC BOOKS

The Golden Age of Canadian Comics was from 1942 to 1946 and was a result of the War Exchange Conservation Act, which did not allow "fiction periodicals" into Canada. This included comic books. Canadian kids needed fun reading and so a purely Canadian comic book industry sprung up. It was successful while there was no competition from the US, but once the war was over and Superman and his pals were flying across the border again, the Canadian Whites, as our comics were known, could not compete.

It was an amazing time when *Nelvana of the Northern Lights, Johnny Canuck* and *Canada Jack* kept kids cheering and, more importantly, reading!

To read more about the Tourond family's adventures, try *Belle of Batoche*, set in the 1885 North West Rebellion or *Outcasts of River Falls*, a story of life on the road allowances.

Discover Jacqueline's other exciting books at:
"http://www.jacquelineguest.com" www.jacquelineguest.com

ACKNOWLEDGEMENTS

Patrick Tourond for his soldier's memory of the Battle of Ortona. (Miss you, Uncle Pat.)

James Tourond, Dad and Soldier (Wish you'd told me more about 'the old days'.)

Lorraine Tourond, Fabulous Family Historian

Nik Burton, Astute Publisher

Laura Peetoom, Editor Extraordinaire

Tadeusz Glowinski, Translator and Head Librarian of Glowinski's Amazing Library, Olesnica, Poland

Jim Langley, Santa Cruz, CA, Bicycle Expert

Nik Richbell, Canadian Pacific Archives

Dr. Phil Langill, University of Calgary, Dept. of Astronomy and Physics, Director of Rothney Astrophysical Observatory

John Bell, Comic Book King

Nipper Guest, Old Soldier and Researcher

Iris Stout, Well Read Wise Woman

Joey Sayer, Calgary Public Library Comic Book Authority

Iris Sadownik, Crescent Heights High School Archivist

Eda Czarnecki and her *Aunt Bozena*, Polish polishers

And a host of others too numerous to name!

ABOUT THE AUTHOR

JACQUELINE GUEST is the author of more than a dozen novels for young readers, many of them award winners, including two previous Coteau Books titles – *The Outcasts of River Falls* and *Ghost Messages*.

Nine of Jacqueline's books have been honoured with Canadian Children's Book Centre Our Choice Awards, and in 2012 she won two American Indian Youth Literature Awards. *Ghost Messages* is a Moonbeam Gold Medal winner and a nominee for both the R. Ross Annett Award and the 2012 Silver Birch® Award in the OLA Forest of Reading® program. *Belle of Batoche* was an Ontario Library Association Best Bet Selection and won the Edmonton Schools Best of the Best Award. Jacqueline's books have also received nominations for the Red Cedar, R. Ross Annett, Hackmatack, Golden Eagle, and Arthur Ellis Mystery Awards.

Jacqueline's works are well-known for having main characters who come from different ethnic backgrounds including First Nations, Inuit or Metis. In 2013, she was awarded the Indspire Award in recognition of her outstanding career achievement.

Alberta born and raised, Jacqueline Guest lives and writes in a cabin in the pine woods of the Rocky Mountain foothills. Robert's brothers in *The Comic Book War* are based on her father and his two brothers.

MIX
Paper from
responsible sources
FSC® C016245

ENVIRONMENTAL BENEFITS STATEMENT

Coteau Books saved the following resources by printing the pages of this book on chlorine free paper made with 100% post-consumer waste.

TREES	WATER	ENERGY	SOLID WASTE	GREENHOUSE GASES
13 FULLY GROWN	**6,294** GALLONS	**6** MILLION BTUs	**421** POUNDS	**1,160** POUNDS

Environmental impact estimates were made using the Environmental Paper Network Paper Calculator 3.2. For more information visit www.papercalculator.org.